THE PLEASURE PRINCIPLE

THE PLEASURE PRINCIPLE

THE AMARYLLIS BOOK
OF EROTIC STORIES

Edited by

G. Sampath

AMARYLLIS

AMARYLLIS

Copyright © Amaryllis, an imprint of Manjul Publishing House Pvt. Ltd.

AMARYLLIS

An imprint of Manjul Publishing House Pvt. Ltd.
• 7/32, Ground Floor, Ansari Road, Daryaganj, New Delhi 110 002
Website: www.manjulindia.com

Registered Office:
10, Nishat Colony, Bhopal 462 003 - India

Distribution Centres:
Ahmedabad, Bengaluru, Bhopal, Kolkata, Chennai,
Hyderabad, Mumbai, New Delhi, Pune

ISBN: 978-93-81506-80-6

This edition first published in 2016

Printed and bound in India by
Thomson Press (India) Ltd.

Contents

Introduction vii

Sexboy 1
Taslima Nasrin

The Baker of Milna 15
Kristen Cosby

Harsingar 37
Amitava Kumar

Naked Cleaning Lady 49
Jaishree Misra

The Degradation of Erasmo S. 65
Cyrus Mistry

The Middle-East Position 89
Krishna Shastri Devulapalli

Insomnia 105
Mitali Saran

The Last House 115
Rupa Bajwa

Thy Will Be Done 127
Shinie Antony

The Holy Sex Tape Project 137
Meena Kandasamy

Graveyard Shift 151
Kankana Basu

First Kiss 163
Vikram Kapur

The House Help 179
Tabish Khair

Chunni Lal 189
Aditya Sharma

The Real Sex 217
Amrita Chatterjee

About the Contributors 225

Introduction

It gives me great pleasure to introduce this collection of erotic stories. I never thought that one day my name would appear on the cover of a book that's primarily about people having sex. Neither did my mother. She still doesn't know.

You might be wondering what qualifies me to edit an anthology such as this. Am I a writer of erotica? No. Am I a professional editor of fiction anthologies? No. Perhaps I am an extremely erotic person? Er... well, my wife may not agree.

To be sure, like most men of my age, I have had my share of erotic experiences. But I wouldn't say they are in the Lady Chatterley league. Or in any league that counts. In fact, my most distinctive erotic memory is a fairly innocuous one.

I was quite young then, late teens. Sexual experience zero. I was in a garment shop, looking to buy a shirt. Helping me pick one was a young Tibetan saleswoman. Slim-waisted, high cheekbones, white shirt, blue jeans.

I finally settled on a dark grey semi-formal. I was in a T-shirt. They did not have a trial room. I was wondering if I should risk buying without trying it on when she said, 'Come here.'

Before I knew it she was behind me, guiding my arms, manhandling me gently, until I found myself inside the shirt. I wasn't expecting this. But she surprised me again. She came close, so close that I could feel her breath, and ran her hands down my chest, smoothening the folds of the fabric. I suddenly felt hot.

She began to fasten the buttons, one by one, starting under my chin. Her hair, lustrous, black, and fragrant, fluttered inches from my lips. I was taller than she was. The top two buttons of her shirt were open. I looked down, and then away in panic.

Her soft hands hovered over my shirt front, now alighting on my chest, only to take flight and come to rest a few centimetres lower, to thrust a rounded hardness into a tiny hole. She had no idea what she was doing – doing to me, that is. Or maybe she did. As her fingers glided down my body, my nerves thrummed in a sweet tingle I had not known before. It was all new to me, and too pleasant to understand.

Once she was done with the buttons, she stepped back to look at me. Then she came up close again, to straighten the collar. I felt her fingers graze my neck, then brush away a thread or a speck of dust from my shoulder. At that moment, had she asked, I would have bought every single shirt in the shop.

In the end, I bought three. I couldn't get her off my mind. I went back the next day, and several times in the subsequent weeks and months. But I never saw her again. I don't remember her face anymore, nor even the name of the shop. But I remember the flowery lightness of her fingers on my body, my chest, my belly. Technically, her touch would not even qualify as touch – for it was through two layers of fabric. And yet, it is to this stranger that I owe my initiation into the erotic.

To be honest, it wasn't until I began writing this Introduction that I even framed that experience as 'erotic'. It doesn't make sense in any other way – I wasn't in love with her. Nor was I sexually attracted. And for the record, she was 'dressing' me and not undressing me. It was simply two random bodies coming in momentary contact to produce a spark of pleasure. A pleasure that is pure gift. An unasked for, unexplained, unexpected giving.

Why did this salesgirl act as she did? Was she having some fun? Was it a desperate tactic to make a sale? Or was she oblivious to the effects she was causing in me? It is all a mystery to me – as it should be. It is my contention that the erotic is the only realm of the mysterious that remains unconquered. Everything else has been analysed, explained, and converted into data. But the erotic is still pure subjectivity. A belt can turn someone mad with lust while for another, it's just a piece of leather to keep the pants up.

Erotic subjectivity typically expresses itself through play. Role play and fantasy are what imbue the ordinary with mystery, inducing the defamiliarisation that is integral to the erotic as well as to literature. If literature originated in day-dreaming and fantasy, it stands to reason that the earliest literature would be of the erotic kind. And so it is. For instance, the first novels in English – by Daniel Defoe, Samuel Richardson, Henry Fielding – had a good deal of prurient content. Today these men are considered, individually and collectively, the 'father' of the English novel. Their novels are 'classics' taught in respectable university departments.

So I have always been puzzled by people who consider erotica to be lowbrow, something 'serious' writers wouldn't have time for. The pseudo-snobs who say, let the EL Jameses of the world do erotic fiction – I want to slap them with this anthology.

For this very reason, there are no 'erotic specialists' in this collection. All are writers with a serious amount of literary work behind them. A couple had written erotic fiction before; most hadn't – until I contacted them. And I wanted it that way.

Many of the writers I approached had a problem writing a made-to-order erotic story. It's one thing for a story to organically develop into an erotic narrative, and quite another to set out to write an avowedly erotic story. While the skill and imagination involved might be the same, the latter is infinitely more difficult. It's like meeting a comedian at a party and asking him to be funny – it doesn't quite work like that.

But the alternative to commissioning erotic stories is to take what's already been written, either stories or novel excerpts. But this book wasn't about collecting existing literature – it was about putting together fresh writing. And that's what you will find here.

Typically, anthology editors are driven by a pre-ordained set of concerns, such as diversity of themes and voices, gender parity in representation of writers, and so on. But I have attempted nothing of the sort. I think *The Pleasure Principle* is fairly diverse without my having had to make an effort to make it so.

On the gender front, if anything, we have surpassed the benchmark by some margin – the book has six male writers and nine female. That we reached this ratio without a self-conscious balancing act is revealing. It suggests that the erotic is primarily, though not exclusively, the realm of the female. I'm not the only one to think so. In her classic essay, 'The Uses of the Erotic,' Audre Lorde writes, 'The erotic is a resource within each of us that lies in a deeply female and spiritual plane, firmly rooted in the power of our unexpressed or unrecognised feeling.'

Lorde, of course, is interested in the political expression of the erotic. My focus, as the editor of this anthology, has been the literary expression of the erotic. But whichever way one looks at it, there is no getting away from the fundamentally destabilising power of eroticism. As Lorde says of our erotic selves, 'We have been taught to suspect this resource, vilified, abused, and devalued within Western society.' Here the 'we' refers to women. But one could say the same for men, and her judgment applies to semi-Westernised societies like India as well.

So if the erotic has been suppressed in our lives, what has taken its place? The pornographic. From the internet to Bollywood to the kind of graphics that accompany news stories, the pornographic is one of the defining elements of popular culture today. It would be no exaggeration to say that for millions of people, pornography mediates their sexuality, and their relationship to their own bodies and the bodies of their lovers. For Lorde, 'pornography is a direct denial of the power of the erotic, for it represents the suppression of true feeling. Pornography emphasizes sensation without feeling'.

This distinction between the erotic and the pornographic has been a guiding principle in the curation of the stories for this book. My brief to the writers was simple: etch out the emotional landscape of sex in a fictional narrative. They liked it for the obvious reason that it offered a broad canvas for the imagination. It partly explains the rich diversity of approach, style, voice, theme, setting, and characters in these stories.

For instance, I did not plan to have a lesbian-themed story, nor did I plan for a homo-erotic one, or a transgender narrative – all of which my friends told me I must specifically commission in order to make the book suitably inclusive. While inclusiveness defined in political terms is important, it is not as if the erotic realm of heterosexuality has been exhausted.

Quite a few of the stories in *The Pleasure Principle* cover new ground even in 'straight' territory. The unexpected transmutations of online lust when it goes offline, the sex tapes of our ancient gods, the yearnings of an elderly widower, the forbidden desires of a middle-aged school teacher – are some of the erotic sub-themes explored in the following narratives.

One question that pops up in the context of an erotic fiction anthology is that of political correctness. My answer to this question: No. In this, I take my inspiration from one of my favourite essayists, Siri Hustvedt. In 'A Plea for Eros', Hustvedt states an obvious truth that a political correctness gone rogue makes us deny: 'Of course women are sexual objects; so are men.' And if this is so, it's because 'desire is always between a subject and an object'. This doesn't mean a free pass for sexual abuse or harassment. But in a context of intimacy between two people, 'erotic pleasure… thrives on the paradox that only by keeping alive the strangeness of that other person can eroticism last'.

Keeping alive this strangeness requires not only objectification, but also imagination, and here we come full circle back to literature – via fantasy – as the treasure house, refuge, and training ground for the imagination.

So, as I have already said, and don't mind saying it again: leave your shoes of political correctness at the door before you enter the portals of literature, especially erotic literature.

Some of the authors in this volume would be familiar to you, some others not so familiar. That's by design. I don't see the point of an anthology that does not make an effort to discover and introduce fresh voices to a wider readership. So

I've aimed for a reasonable mix of established and upcoming talents.

Being by nature allergic to rules or expectations of any kind, I have broken even the easiest and most obvious expectation to fulfil – of picking only Indian (or Indian-origin) writers for an Indian anthology being brought out by an Indian publisher for an Indian readership. I have included a white American writer from San Francisco for no reason or logic whatsoever other than the fact that I loved her story.

Before I conclude my ramblings, I feel obliged to answer one final query: the why question. Why an anthology of erotic stories? Why now? Aren't there enough of them already?

I believe what India needs right now, more than anything else – more than foreign investment, more than good governance, and more than nine percent economic growth or a half-decent football team – is a new volume of erotic stories. And more and more of them. India needs an erotic revolution. Indians need to give up both TV channel spirituality and Redtube pornography – which sort of nicely complement each other – and get back in tune with the physicality of their bodies, with the geography of their feelings.

Lorde's definition of the erotic is most relevant in this context. 'The erotic,' she writes, 'is a measure between the beginnings of our sense of self and the chaos of our strongest feelings.' Pornography reigns supreme today because nobody – neither the powers that circumscribe our life choices, nor we as individuals – are ready to engage with the chaos of our feelings. Those of you who work in offices would be familiar with the managerial injunction to 'keep feelings out of it', or to 'decide rationally and not emotionally'. The erotic is all about putting emotions and feelings back where they belong – in our lives. And what better place to begin than the domain where feelings are being vacuumed out by pornography: the bedroom?

So yes, I might as well come out and say it: for me, this anthology of erotic fiction is not only a literary but also a political project. It is my claim that bringing out a collection of erotic stories today, especially in today's India – I don't need to explain what I mean here – is an act of moral responsibility.

I, therefore, wish to thank all the writers who took the trouble to ration the time and energy for contributing a story. A big thank you also to the publisher Amaryllis for being ever-supportive and patient, and giving me a free hand as an editor – a rarity in these times.

Putting this volume together has been a great journey of discovery for me, one that began last March, and is ending nearly a year later. Yours as a reader will begin now, as you turn the page. Or maybe you are one of those who reads the Introduction last – after having read the stories, which is not a bad idea I must say. Either way, I hope you will love the stories, not just with your mind, but your body too. Welcome to *The Pleasure Principle*.

G. Sampath
April, 2016
New Delhi

Sexboy

TASLIMA NASRIN

Translated from Bangla by Arunava Sinha

CHAITALI IS WAITING for Sexboy. As evening lands in Calcutta, so will Sexboy. Holding hands with the darkness, Sexboy's taxi from Dum Dum Airport will enter this south Calcutta lane. He's coming from Bombay. He's going to stay with Chaitali. The two of them have done almost everything over the past six months, just not met face to face. They had spoken for the first time on Facebook, primarily about sex. Chaitali had been attracted by the name Sexboy. The profile picture was of a naked man's. What else could the conversation be about except sex! It was to talk about sex that Chaitali had added him. Her own barren existence, devoid of sex, was becoming unbearable. So many young men in the city, and yet a beautiful, accomplished woman like Chaitali couldn't find herself a lover. But then how would she, for she did none of the things required to get one.

Chaitali couldn't stand the city these days. She was invited to parties, but she didn't go. Seeing the same faces, listening to the same stories a hundred times, saying hello with an artificial smile dangling from her lips – Chaitali had had enough of all this. Social networks threw up fresh faces, new conversations.

Chaitali's father had chosen the man she used to be married to. Several years had passed since she had divorced Subrata. It wasn't as though nothing had developed between her and other people since then. Chaitali had had a relationship lasting nearly a month with a colleague ten years younger. But she was forced to break up after Ashok got married. Chaitali had not wanted him to sleep with her in secret while his young wife languished at home.

Chaitali works for an English newspaper. A long-standing job, with many responsibilities. But Chaitali doesn't like bringing work home. She wants to be free of worries in her own house. You have to put aside a little time for yourself – time is short in any case. Her daughter studies in Delhi. Chaitali has to make enquiries about her too. It's easy to keep track in the age of the mobile phone. The office is just an office, it will continue functioning with or without Chaitali. And her daughter has an independent life. She will adjust easily if Chaitali were to die. Chaitali's own parents were dead. She was their only child. But she doesn't even remember much of them anymore.

Earlier she would settle down with a book when she came back home from work, now it's with Facebook. Fatal attraction. Actually it's not to Facebook, but to reading what Sexboy tells her every day – all the things he will do with her in bed, how he will kiss her all over her body, how he will kiss her on her mouth and her breasts, how he will taste Chaitali, and give her frequent orgasms. This addiction has released her from her restlessness. She no longer looks at the young men in her office or on the road with hungry eyes. Sexboy has provided much of what was missing from Chaitali's everyday life. She is grateful to him.

The relationship is no longer limited to Facebook. For two months they have been talking on the phone almost every day, and over the past few days they have even had sex over Skype.

Virtual sex. Sexboy's real name is Vijay, a thirty-five-year-old Marathi architect. Can there be a better couple? It was Chaitali who had proposed having actual sex with Vijay. She had emailed him a Bombay-Calcutta-Bombay ticket. When he got the ticket, Vijay had leapt up, saying, 'Let's fuck the entire week.' Chaitali wants to touch Vijay. She wanted real lovemaking, a flesh and blood body, she no longer cares for masturbation.

Chaitali has taken leave for a week. Just this afternoon Ashok asked her, 'A week's leave? Going somewhere?'

Chaitali had answered with a smile, 'I've booked a flight to cloud nine. Want to come?'

'I definitely would have if I hadn't got married.'

Chaitali had a small smile on her lips. 'Thank heavens you got married,' she said in her head. Chaitali no longer feels her old attraction for Ashok; Vijay has taken his place, she doesn't know when it happened.

Vijay was the kind of man Chaitali had needed in her life after Ashok got married, a torrent, who would sweep away all the old memories like flotsam, make her glow brighter with a new passion, as though she had just been born, as though she had never had anything like a past.

Gazing at her for a while, Ashok had asked, 'Have you fallen in love? You look so radiant.'

With a sweet smile, Chaitali had asked, 'How's Muna, tell me. Everything alright?' She had left without waiting for an answer. A little earlier than she usually did.

Vijay reigned all over her body now, a high tide running through it.

After returning home she has been singing in the shower. She doesn't usually spend so much time bathing. She has done herself up with great care, put on some perfume, and changed the bedspread, adding two pillows to the two already on the bed. She lives in a stately old house. The drawing room, dining room, and kitchen are downstairs, and the four bedrooms upstairs. One of them is stuffed with things that are inessential, or might become essential in future. Chaitali occupies one. Another one is for guests, while Shakuntala lives in the fourth one. Shakuntala has worked here as a domestic help for a long time. She's been here since birth, her mother used to work here earlier. Shakuntala asks, 'Is Ashok-babu coming, Chaiti? You're dressing up.'

Chaitali replies irritably, 'What rubbish, Didi, Ashok is happily married, why should he come?'

'Who's the new Mr Fortunate?'

'You'll see,' Chaitali smiles.

Shakuntala has cooked up a storm today. Vijay and Chaitali will have a candle-lit dinner. Then they will go into the bedroom and lock the door. Chaitali has drawn the curtains open. From the bed they will see the moon lighting up the sky. The room will fill with moonlight, and they will bathe by it, immersing their bodies all night in each other's. The room is fragrant with jasmine. It's like a festival of flowers. She put some Rabindra sangeet on. Kanika. The song 'My heart's wish is fulfilled' plays. Chaitali sings along. She could never sing very well, but she pours her heart and soul into Kanika's songs. Songs sung from the heart sound lovely even without a voice meant for singing or holding notes perfectly.

Chaitali has dressed in a blue sari. She has deliberately chosen a deep-cut blouse. Her breasts are peeping out. Let them. Chaitali's hair is L'Oréal black. There's only a hint of grey, but she has wiped away its signs. A tight body at forty and ageing hair don't go together. Not that she has any objection to wisps of grey. But she plans to spend an intimate week with Sexboy, why let signs of ageing intrude?

Vijay had called as soon as he had landed. Chaitali puts a bottle of Black Label and two glasses on the bedside table. She has never had an adventure like this before. Nor has she felt such arousal. She meets a stranger on Facebook, and then both of them make arrangements for a sexual relationship, no love involved, no one says I love you, no discussion about anything in the world besides sex. But neither feels as though they're doing anything reprehensible. Both are adults. Both live alone. Neither is cheating on a husband or wife. If their bodies desire one another, why should they not sleep together?

Her body has been flowing, liquid, since morning. Chaitali feels as though she is a girl of sixteen. What if she IS sixteen? At sixteen she has read difficult books which people read at forty or fifty. If she has a chance to reclaim her sixteen, why shouldn't she? She has not vowed not to go back to an earlier time in her life.

Vijay is probably nothing but an enormous penis to Chaitali. He has told her he is coming specifically to sleep with her. A relationship has grown based strictly on physical attraction. Who says it always has to be the heart before the body, she asks herself, it's much more logical for the body to come before the heart. Vijay will definitely put his arm around her and kiss her deeply as soon as she opens the door. Then straight to the bedroom. Chaitali pictures the scene, closing her eyes with passion. Currents of pleasure moan quietly within her body. She has instructed Shakuntala to be in her own room with the door shut, Chaitali will call her if needs be. Shakuntala knows

the rules. This was how it was with Ashok. She had often told
Chaitali after her divorce, 'Time you got married, Chaiti.'
Chaitali had spent several years in refusal. Then, during her
relationship with Ashok, Shakuntala had said, 'Get yourself a
permanent friend.' Despite her best efforts, Chaitali had been
unable to convince Shakuntala that you cannot turn someone
into something of your own just because you want to. Shakuntala
has been with her since Chaitali was born. She hasn't married.
And yet she cannot stop worrying about Chaitali's not getting
married or not having a long-term companion. This is probably
what happens when your mistress's family is more important to
you than yourself.

2

Vijay arrives. He's different from the way she had visualised
him from his photographs or Skype videos. He's taller than she
had thought, slimmer too, and even more handsome than she
had imagined. They shake hands, saying hi Vijay, hi Chaitali.
Instead of the bedroom, Chaitali leads him into the drawing
room. They sit down face to face on sofas. A quick exchange of
glances. Easy smiles on both their faces. Chaitali waits to find
out whether Vijay will say, just as he did on Skype, 'You look
so hot, honey. Come on, let's have sex.' Vijay would take off his
clothes on his own, lowering the camera to point to his groin.
Chaitali would also uncover her breasts. Vijay says nothing of
the sort today. Still, a sexually charged couple is sitting opposite
each other right now. The desires of their bodies are about to
be fulfilled.

But, how strange, there's nothing sexual in their conversation.
– May I have some water?

– I'm sorry, I should have offered you some. Would you like some tea or coffee?

– No, I don't drink either.

– Whiskey then?

– I don't drink whiskey at all.

– I see. What time do you have dinner?

– No fixed time. Your room is so beautifully done up. Whom do all these books belong to? Are they yours?

– Yes, they are.

Rising, Vijay goes up to the books and examines them raptly. A long time passes. He drinks the water Chaitali brings him without taking his eyes off the books.

– If you don't mind, may I take some of these out?

– Of course, go right ahead.

Vijay picks three books and leafs through them. Returning to the sofa, he says, I see you like Roddy Doyle too. Have you read *The Dead Republic*?

I've read just three of his, says Chaitali with a smile, *Paddy Clark Ha Ha Ha*, *A Star Called Henry*, and *The Guts*.

– You have a brilliant collection.

– Quite a few classics in there.

– Never mind the classics. I've read them as a child. If I have Bill Bryson I need no one else these days.

– I have several books of his.

Vijay's face lights up with happiness.

– You like Bill Bryson too? Tell me which of his books you have. I haven't read his latest yet.

– My favourite is *A Short History of Nearly Everything*.

– It's unique.

– I have *I'm A Stranger Here Myself*, *At Home*, *Neither Here Nor There*...

– *One Summer* isn't out yet, is it?

– This October.

A little boy lives inside Vijay. Chaitali is pleased when she observes this. He starts glowing from time to time, just like her. Vijay loses himself in the conversation about books. As though they belong to a book club. Chaitali's taste in books has never matched with anyone's so closely. Then the conversation moves to travel, and they compare notes on which parts of the country they've visited. Here too they converge as they describe their respective experiences, telling each other of the mountains and the waterfalls and the forests that have enthralled them the most. Then the subject of food comes up, and here again they are similar. Both of them like Bengali food.

They keep chatting as the clock signals ten o'clock. Neither of them drinks anything but water. Chaitali calls Shakuntala, who lays the food on the table. No, Chaitali sees no need to light candles. Vijay says as he eats, 'Perfect, low on oil and spices. Just like my mother's cooking.' Shakuntala is a good cook. Vijay heaps praises on her. He serves Chaitali. When he has finished, he washes his plate in the kitchen himself. A complete gentleman. Chaitali likes this. She hasn't seen a man like him in Calcutta. Vijay says he will take Chaitali out to dinner tomorrow, to Calcutta's best restaurant for Bengali food. Shakuntala asks whether Vijay's mother cooks only Marathi food, or Bengali food too. After a long silence, Vijay says his mother died a year ago. In a road accident. Vijay used to live with her. His brother had got married and moved out. Vijay was driving that night. They were on their way back home from dinner at his brother's place in Bandra. He had had a few drinks. A truck was hurtling towards them like a missile, he hadn't seen it at all.

The truck had hit them, and the car had rolled into a ditch. His mother had died on the spot. Vijay had been injured too, but he had recovered after a couple of days in hospital. Vijay had not had a drink since that day. The subject of one mother leads to the other. Shakuntala joins in the conversation about Chaitali's mother. Chaitali had forgotten her a long time ago. Today her mother is revisiting her. Everyone unlocks their bank of recollections. Their eyes moisten as they walk into the mist of memories. Chaitali would probably have remained oblivious of her mother had Vijay not mentioned his own. It is past midnight. 'Where am I sleeping?' asks Vijay.

Chaitali thinks for a minute. Then she tells Shakuntala with a smile, 'Can you make the bed in the guestroom? Change the sheets. There are extra pillows in my bedroom, take them.'

Vijay has never been to Calcutta before. 'I'll take you to the Indian Museum tomorrow, and Marble Palace,' Chaitali tells him. 'You'll enjoy these places.'

Picking up Bill Bryson's *At Home*, Vijay asks with a sweet smile, 'May I take this to read at night? I haven't read it.'

3

Chaitali and Vijay roam the streets of the city like teenagers during his stay in Calcutta, caring neither about the rain or storms nor the scorching sun. From street food to speciality restaurants, they omit nothing. They take rides in hand-drawn rickshaws, in boats on the river, losing themselves where they please. There is a strange joy in aimless wandering, even things not worth noticing catch the eye. Chaitali has been born and has grown up in Calcutta. And yet, in seeing the city afresh with Vijay, she discovers many things she didn't know. Many aromas she has never breathed in. Vijay is a curious person. He examines everything closely, even soaps himself and bathes with urchins at the roadside tap under the burning sun. In the Tiljala slums he not only chats with people but actually makes a friend or two. Chaitali forgets her job, her daughter, her past, her future. She seems to be at a distance from the world, beyond everyone's reach, up in an unfamiliar sky. This is probably what the real cloud nine is like. Vijay has gifted Shakuntala two magnificent Dhaka silk saris. She claims never to have dressed in such wonderful saris in her life. A Jogen Chowdhury painting for Chaitali. She tells Vijay a great deal about her life. About her divorce, her daughter, Ashok, a gathering of joys and sorrows. Vijay listens quietly. He talks to her too, but he prefers listening. Vijay grows close to her in just a few days. As though he is her childhood friend. As though Chaitali has played hopscotch and marbles with him as a child and as an adolescent, gone fishing with him and played with tops. Sometimes Chaitali's eyes brim with tears as she recounts an incident from the past. Vijay holds her lightly and calms her down. This is all the physical contact she has with him during the week. Once or twice she wants to kiss him, but stops herself.

Vijay leaves, having given Chaitali the best time of her life. She does not get the opportunity to ask why Vijay's persona behind the profile of Sexboy on Facebook is the complete opposite of his real life character. She does not ask, but she assumes that it is to escape from the searing grief and depression after his mother's death that Vijay has resorted to his Facebook personality. But why has Chaitali taken refuge in Facebook? She has no grief, no depression. Perhaps there's something within her that she herself is not aware of. Is Vijay aware? She hasn't asked. Chaitali has felt no tide in her body this past week. It has only rained in her heart. Is her Facebook persona not the real Chaitali? Which Vijay is the real one, wonders Chaitali. Is it the one she meets on the Net, or the flesh and blood one she has met in Calcutta? The real-life Vijay is also Sexboy on Facebook, with whom she celebrates physicality every night. So many mysteries lie within a single individual. Perhaps several people occupy the same person, each one different from the other. Is it impossible to have all of them at the same time? Must you lose one to get another? Chaitali confronts Chaitali with this question. Chaitali the journalist, Chaitali the mother, Chaitali the daughter, Chaitali on Facebook, the Chaitali who talks to Shakuntala – none of them resembles any of the others. But why should one Chaitali have to retreat when another one comes to the forefront? Can human beings not register more than one self in every person, and therefore present only one of their many selves to others? What is threatened if more than one self is offered at the same time? Is it tradition, or society, or one's own hidden anxieties and the fear of rejection? Chaitali wonders about all of this on her way home after seeing Vijay off at the airport. She is gazing absently out of the window when the SMS arrives.

Vijay has written, I love you.

Chaitali's heart trembles. A deep pleasure spreads from her heart across her body.

Chaitali writes, me too.

When she returns home, the CD with Kanika's songs is still playing. 'Don't leave me, my eternal friend…' Chaitali sings along.

The Baker of Milna

KRISTEN COSBY

ANTONIO FERRERA II exited his patisserie well after dark and turned towards the house of his mistress. He'd scrubbed the storefront and locked the door to the storeroom, where he'd left croissant dough rising on the counters, sweets covered and awaiting display in the morning. His son, Antonio Ferrera III, would arrive before dawn to begin the morning baking and open the shop.

Since the boy had come of age, father and son had shared the responsibilities of the pastry shop equally, alternating days. The father worked while his son slept, or sat on a bench out front drinking coffee in the shade, and vice-versa.

Antonio Ferrera II's knees ached. His back ached. The beauty and virility of his Italian lineage lent itself to a heavy-set build when fed with pastry dough, but he still had a full head of hair, deep pewter grey, and an eager squid between his legs. One of discerning tastes and hungers.

He tucked a small box of marzipans under his arm.

The street was deserted except for a few amorous stray cats. He paused for a moment to let the harbour air wash over him. The sea licked quietly at the quay. A person could walk straight from his front door across the street and into the water. No barrier, no lip. Boats tied up street side, their hulls tapping against the stones.

Across from his shop, a small sailboat rocked to a different rhythm, the mast yawing in wider and wider arcs. From under a tented sail, the youthful cries of the two aboard undulated towards him. A duet, swelling. After the final crescendo, Antonio turned away from the water, and walked two blocks northward and three blocks eastward. The whitewashed buildings and colourful paper lanterns of the waterfront gave way to grey stucco walls, and dark narrow streets.

He stopped at the door of his mistress, the imaginative Zsuzsa, a Hungarian widow who'd washed up in Milna several years before with a tale about a disappeared husband that he'd never quite believed. She was an excellent storyteller.

Her door was opened to the night breeze. She sat at her kitchen table beneath a naked incandescent bulb. The smoke of her cigarette curled towards the light. Her peroxide bleached hair was in a French twist that hid most, but not quite all, of her grey strands. She was not a natural blonde. He did not care. The contrast of upstairs and downstairs pleased him – something for him to know and other men to guess about. Between her belly button and the coarse black forest surrounding her sex were three lonely hairs. He had names for them: Kristina, Isabella, Maya.

He left a fine cascade of flour behind him as he crossed her floor, and presented her with the small box.

'Dragam,' she purred, rising.

Lying atop the soft bedcovers, he watched her undress and slide next to him. He walked his fingers over the soft sands of her abdomen, swerved right to avoid her navel, and continued north. Her room was a study of old-world taste – every surface snow-capped with lace and besotted with porcelain figurines. But the lush heart of her house was her large bed, and its red velvet and mahogany headboard. Quite strong. Elemental to whatever Zsuzsa's imagination improvised.

That evening, he told her of the small boat yawing in the harbour, of the lapping waves. His requests were precise: 'Pretend we have little time, pretend we might be caught. First I will stand. You will kneel. After, I want you to make the sound of a young girl with a boy atop her who is making a boat rock.'

Zsuzsa had two superb skills.

The first: with her mouth around his member she moved her tongue in opposition to the pull of her lips. Pausing at the top, waiting seconds, while his back arched, his hips beseeched, and he hiccupped air as if he'd forgotten how to breathe.

The second: She had a knack for tightening her cleft around his organ and holding it, so that he fit and filled her perfectly while the whole hot earth stood still.

Afterwards, he settled next to her and then, as usual, requested his second and third pleasures of the evening: 'A cigarette, please, and a story.'

If arousing enough, they would begin again.

'Display my curve, and the three girls as you speak,' he said, lighting a second cigarette for her.

'Certainly, Dragam.'

'Make it a good tale. I'm distracted by my son. He's been staying later at the shop, hiding from his mother. He disappears all night and is tired all day.'

'Perhaps he has a girl?'

Antonio snorted. 'He is too quiet to get a girl.'

'But he has your looks.'

Antonio grunted.

'Never mind, Dragam. Think of other things.'

'Tell me a story of young love. I want an American. And a captain.'

Zsuzsa lit another cigarette. 'Then I must tell you of *Kapetan* and Zoltan's American nanny.'

'Zoltan? A friend of yours?' Antonio asked, tweaking her left breast. Despite the pull of gravity on her ample curves, her skin was taut, resilient, and smooth — that of a woman ten or fifteen years her junior, and her body, a pleasing contrast of youthfulness and experience.

'On the contrary. This Zoltan had made a fortune importing rare and delicate furs of young animals and bought a small motor yacht that he kept in Portorose. Once a year, he piled his wife and two children aboard and pretended to know how to operate it. The children were very spoiled. For his two little terrors, Zoltan had decided to hire an American nanny, one who spoke no Hungarian, so that the children might learn unaccented English. Thus, he hired Carolyn from Carolina.

'Carolyn had come to Budapest as the travelling companion of one of his colleagues' niece and had been persuaded to take the job. A girl from a small American village, just shy of nineteen, and easily dazzled by glamour.'

'A beautiful buxom girl? If so, put me in the story too.'

'For you, Édesem, my sweetness, I will make her young and beautiful. If you promise to pay attention...

'This Carolyn of Carolina had spent a childhood praying for beauty. Until that very moment, when she'd boarded Zoltan's boat, her face had been a bit too round and her nose a bit too big. A tendency to be *telt*, as we say in Hungarian, a little bit fleshy in these skinny times. Monet and Marai would have salivated to paint her, but boys her own age had never paid her a whit of attention. Being passed over in favour of pretty girls had left her a little bitter, a little prudish. She'd been seduced by one much older friend of the family and one aggressive classmate, who'd given her little pleasure or confidence.

'When she stepped off Zoltan's boat in Milna, befuddled from seasickness, she was succulent as ripe peach. Her nectar filled the air, trailing behind her down the street, advertising her readiness for plucking. But she had no idea what a morsel she was. She had just learned that Croatian men whistle when a young lady wears a skirt that ends above the knees. She'd just learned that, in Hungarian, *dragam* means precious and *édesem* means my sweet. But she hadn't learnt to throw her shoulders back or swing her hips, or to gather the resulting howls of delight. She did not know that one day, it would all stop just as suddenly as it had started.

'Carolyn stared open-mouthed at the sleek tourists prowling the waterfront – unaccustomed to the sing-song of Croatian, or to the push-pull of your narrow streets around this hot little vulva of a harbour.

'She had only one dress, a short blue frock with a black lace overlay. That was part of her appeal, the blonde virginal quality of her face, the cocktail dress worn proudly, without irony, midday.'

Antonio Ferrera II stroked the soft curve of Zsuzsa's bottom.

'Back to the baker. Antonio the Baker. Where is he?'

'Varya, Dragam, just wait… The Antonio of this story is also impatient, as was his father before him. He was two blocks away on the other side of the boardwalk, sitting outside his father's patisserie, smoking his fifth cigarette of the day. He was eighteen years old – stocky, a bit short, but bull-strong. Dressed in baker's whites, his clothes contrasted sharply with his thick, jet-black hair, and the swarthy, striking features of his Italian-Croatian visage. He had the most beautiful face in Milna, or perhaps on the whole island of Brac. With those wide almond eyes, and wrestler's shoulders that tapered into his narrow-waisted pants, he made women of all ages smile and imagine settling back against flour sacks with his strong arms around them.

'That morning he looked a bit haggard and nervous. His rotation in the patisserie had just ended. His father was now at the counter. The boy was sitting outside the door of the patisserie on a low wooden bench next to a grey-haired bloke in a sailor's cap.

'Antonio bounced his foot nervously, and as he did, a cascade of flour sifted from the cuffs of his pants.

'"Don't worry. They will like her," the grizzled sailor said.

'Soon people would begin to gather at the door, but for the moment, there was only Antonio and the man seated beside him, and the rattle of his father fussing about the shop. The old sailor was known to the boy simply as *Kapetan*. His ship, a small red pilot boat, came and went from Milna irregularly. Kapetan was fond of espresso laden with sugar. Our young baker was happy to make strong coffee in exchange for the captain's imported cigarettes. Together they smoked and watched the tourists rouse and emerge onto the decks of their boats in various states of undress.

'The boy had smoked twice his usual number of cigarettes that morning.

'He'd been awake all night, bent over his worktable in the storeroom of the patisserie. The result was now scandalously displayed in the window of his father's shop. Amidst the usual cookies and cakes stood the torso of a naked woman formed entirely from pastry dough. The torso – head and arms and legs hacked-off in the style of ruined Greek statuary – had its back arched suggestively. Her firm "skin" and full breasts were proudly displayed, nipples erect, the stumps of her limbs flung widely. The statue was nearly life-size and masterfully executed. The abundant curves of breasts and hips and the delicate waist demonstrated a certain amount of naïve romanticism about the properties of the female figure. Yet there was just enough sag to the cleavage and a dimple upon the thighs to indicate that young Antonio had beheld at least one real, nude woman. And though she'd been exquisitely proportioned, she had been far more mature than he.

'The young baker rubbed his eyes. He should return home to bed. But his beloved, the result of many long nights of trial and error, stood, unveiled and vulnerable, in the window. His thumbprints baked into her shoulders and thighs.

'She'd begun as a nipple that rose under his fingers from a mound of sweet bread. Then an entire breast. A pair. A dozen Liliths had crumbled and burnt, before his masterpiece could stand. It had been heartbreaking each time he'd failed. The torsos he'd formed expanded and contracted, living matter that responded to his touch. When at last, one emerged perfectly from the oven, he'd become aroused just by looking at her shape.'

Zsuzsa rolled onto her side and Antonio Ferrara caressed the curve of her hip.

'Antonio's Curve,' he thought, with reverence. Such a curve. So delicious to behold. He nibbled its crest, gently.

She pushed him away.

'Relax, Antonio…'

'Kapetan sat back, handed the boy another cigarette. People were beginning to stop. The boy strained to hear what they said. Mostly, they spoke in English, Italian. He harkened for the tone, the mood, but most of all to keep sight of his beloved. But the crowd around the window blocked his view.

'Just then Kapetan elbowed him.

'"See there," he said in a soft voice.

'Antonio turned towards the harbour and froze.'

'The American?'

'Carolyn.'

'Of Carolina.'

'The same. She lagged behind her employer and his two children. Hot, tired, and hungry. A vegetarian, she missed chocolate and peanut butter – that tongue-slowing American sludge. Her employers, this family of Budapestians, could stomach untold quantities of meat at every meal – long thick salami, slick dabs of pork fat, the rumps of ham and smiling suckling pigs on spits. She cringed at each restaurant table. She'd been living on salad for a month. She'd thought of jumping ship. But on a small Croatian island, where could a foreign girl hide?

'Zoltan stopped at the patisserie window, craning his neck to glimpse what the crowd was ogling. Carolyn paused in the doorway. From inside wafted a breath of the sugar and jam. Salivating, she closed her eyes, drank the sweet air. Her carnivorous employer gave up his quest to push through the crowd at the window and moved down the street, children in tow. Carolyn lagged in the doorway, rapt with hunger.

'Antonio's mouth opened, his nostrils flared. If the scent and taste of the girl standing next to him drifted through the air, he would catch it. Her dress brushed against his knees. He caught the lace hem between his fingers and pulled. Carolyn turned around sharply and looked down.

'Their eyes fastened upon one another.

'The sweet air thickened around them and spun into tufts of sugar. This cloud muffled all the sound, the people, the harbour, the excitement over the statue in the window.

'You know this kind of story, Dragam, it can only happen when lust is fresh and sex is still a novelty. By the time you've had your fourth lover, or your fifth shared orgasm – when you are relatively certain that they can be achieved again, the purity of your urgency fades. It's replaced by many things – endurance, nuance, complexity – but that raw haphazard desire is never quite the same. The body, at eighteen, is primed to fuck – to breathe and eat and fuck.

'Young Antonio's gaze sizzled through Carolyn from eyeballs to toenails, smelting her sandals into the gooey tar. She was stuck.

'Eyes molten, the boy lifted the hem of her skirt to his lips.

'It was too much. Carolyn of Carolina broke the spell, pulled her feet from the tar, and ran after Zoltan.

'Antonio's hand hung midair. He did not chase after her, for he was a shy boy.

'He brought the hand that had touched her dress to his lips, but could taste nothing.

'The old captain watched, smiling. "Bravo, Antonio. Bravo," he purred.'

Antonio Ferrera II walked his fingers along the ridgeline of Zsuzsa's side.

'But where is she going?' he asked. 'And why? Doesn't she see how he desires her?'

'Perhaps she's afraid.'

'Fear is nothing in the face of lust.'

'Fear is everything... fear fuels young lust... fear of loneliness, fear of inadequacy, fear of discovery... what powers fuckery at that age is nerves. Later other fears – such as the scoldings of one's wife.'

Antonio grumbled, 'Back to the young baker.'

'The despondent boy watched Zoltan, the children, and the girl board Zoltan's yacht. Zoltan drew up their small gangplank in preparation for departure.

'Kapetan eyed the harbour and stubbed out his cigarette.

'"I must go," he said quietly, "can you sell me a pound of sugar? My supplies are low."

'Antonio rose lethargically.

'"With a little speed," Kapetan said.

'Our despondent boy elbowed his way through the crowded shop – for it was twice as crowded as usual – to fetch the captain his sugar. Then he went home to bed, still feeling the hem of the blue dress slip between his fingers. He'd lost interest in his statue. He'd lost interest in everything.

'That night, in the patisserie storeroom, sleepless with fresh heartbreak, our young Antonio was attempting a new masterpiece. But the pastry dough was fickle and slid through his fingers like quicksand. Try as he might, he could not sculpt a likeness of the girl in blue, for he had not touched or tasted her body.

'So great was his concentration that he was deaf to the water rippling against the quayside with the licks of a million tongues and the half dozen hulls knocking against the pier.

'So great was his concentration he did not hear the first rap at the patisserie door.

'Nor did he hear the second.

'On the third, he threw down the dough and yanked open the door, red-faced and cross.

'And Carolyn stepped into the lemon yellow light of the shop.

'He touched her hair. He touched her face. And then he lowered his mouth to her bare shoulder.'

'But how?' asked Antonio Ferrera II.

'As Zoltan's ship left the harbour earlier that afternoon, the faintest trace of burnt caramel had wafted above the stink of algae and engine exhaust. Remembering the sticky air around the shop, the gooey pavement, the way her dress had pulled from her body as the beautiful boy tugged its hem, Carolyn had brought her wrist to her lips and kissed herself open-mouthed, tasting her own skin, until the lining of her bathing suit was sodden. And precisely when Carolyn kissed herself, the engine of Zoltan's yacht spluttered, stalled. And refused to start again.'

Antonio Ferrera nodded, satisfied. 'Because lust is the most powerful force on earth.'

Zsuzsa smiled. 'Lust and good timing.'

'Young Antonio led Carolyn to the unlit storeroom where he worked. He paused. The overhead lights would be too bright. He vanished into the dark, lighting old oil lamps and placing them atop his worktable, around which the scent of sugar and vanilla was so thick that you could lick it from the air.

'In the storeroom, Carolyn could see a puddle of flour on the worktable, the flickering reflection of an enormous chrome refrigerator, and dollies stacked with trays and trays of sweets.

'"Oh," Carolyn said, and again. "Oh."

'The tray nearest her paraded rows of marzipan mounds, each topped with a delicate nipple. She popped one into her mouth.

'Antonio grinned. The girl was hungry. And there were so many things to feed her. There were custard cakes that quivered when touched, savoury donuts that bled raspberry or apricot jam when pierced. Tubular cylinders of flakey pastry filled with cream, the pastry of which shattered between his thumb and forefinger when he brought them to her mouth, leaving dapples of whipped milk on her lips. Next, a tray of tiny billowing squares of dough, each with a slit in the middle. (Here, you call them "torn pants" or "torn panties", though they look like the hairless entrance to a woman.)

'The sensibilities of our shy, slightly prudish little American were overwhelmed by the obscenity of the shapes, the variety of flavours, and the sheer abundance of the smorgasbord. Sugar glittered in her veins. When Antonio revealed rows of cookies shaped like peaches, or like tiny bottoms mooning the ceiling, she brought one to her lips and flicked its cleft with her tongue.

'Antonio smiled. He plucked a candied apricot from a box and divaricated one side of its fold with his tongue, inviting her to do the same, just before he closed his mouth over hers.

'Kissing changed their composition.

'He took her upper lip in his mouth and sucked gently, moving next to her nose, her chin, her ear. Licking its lobe, then pushing his tongue deeply into the narrow orifice. Every bit of her skin had been scrubbed and salted by the sea and he grew thirstier with each kiss.

'*A drink?* he motioned. But Carolyn of Carolina didn't understand. She nodded brightly and undid the first button of his uniform.

'Antonio snuffed out the lamps and their shadows tumbled from the walls.

'Under his clothes, under her clothes, their flesh rose, swelling against the constraint of fabric, seeking each other.

'The small buttons down the front of his shirt were slow work for her fingers, now sticky with sweets. Her dress had no buttons, and could easily have been pulled over her head. Instead Antonio rolled one strap and the other off her shoulders, the cloth curling like cinnamon sticks.

'It was too hot in the storeroom.

'He turned her to face the cool metal door of the refrigerator, spread her arms wide, and pressed his body against hers, the condensation in such delicious contrast to the griddle of his torso that she gasped. His hand travelled between her legs, brushing at the lace of her white panties.'

'Do you have such panties?' interrupted Antonio Ferrera II.

'Of course.'

'Put them on.'

'Gladly, Dragam.'

'Now come lie beside me so I can touch them.'

'Shall I continue?'

'Please do.'

'Young Antonio's tongue flitted outside his lips like a garden snake tasting the air. Without touching, he held his palm above the soft pink skin of Carolyn's right nipple and smiled as the areole darkened, tightened, and grew towards his fingertips. He took the breast in his mouth and suckled.

'Perhaps on mornings past when his father entered the shop, he'd flipped his creations over and pressed the front of his pants against the counter to kill his erection. Now, no father, no statues, just Carolyn, and the soft lace of her panties ridging as he rolled them down one thigh and then the other.

'Naked except for her sandals, she was somehow more naked than if she were wearing nothing at all. Darling Antonio boosted her onto his worktable, then knelt and unbuckled each sandal, kissing her ankles, the insides of her knees. He parted her thighs with strong thumbs, kneading upwards. Stroking the paleness of her inner leg, marvelling at its plasticity. How quickly he adapted the press of his thumbs to flesh, careful not to touch her with the calluses on his fingers, or the rough scars where the oven had burned him.

'"Oh," Carolyn murmured again, louder this time, her boldness rising.

'She wrapped her legs around his hipbones, palmed his abdomen and slipped her hand down between cloth and skin to the hot thicket below, finding a smooth handle of flesh, waiting, rigid as a stirring spoon. She teased with her fingertips, unfastened button, zipper, and pushed his garments over his buttocks, and down. He slid her across the worktable towards him. Flour dammed along her legs, creating a soft wave that surfed to the edge of the counter, dusting her sex and thighs, tumbling down the backs of her knees and calves.

'His fingers slipped inside Carolyn. Two, gently, deftly, stirring. The slightly ridged callous on his index finger now working as an advantage. The sap of her gash wetted his hand. She exhaled a ragged breath — almond-scented, sweet. Another. He placed a damp finger against her lips and then against his. This elixir was what he was after, and he wanted her to taste it — her smooth vinegar and whey.

'She dropped a hand into the pool of flour, and placed it on his chest, leaving a print, then took another handful and raked it through his hair.

'He pushed her flat on the table and vanished again. Above her, the hot humid dark was heavy as a blanket. She waited. Patient on the table. Body on the slab. Almost frightened. Suddenly, across the room, he lit a candle, placed it on a tray. The light revealed three white porcelain bowls. The tray levitated. Above the gleaming dishes, a grin flickered.

'Antonio slid an ice cube against her shoulder, and drew slow trails of glacier melt down her arms, along her collarbone, then travelled from her neck to her navel. Pleasant torture. He placed the ice cube in his mouth, and drew his chilled tongue from her navel back to her tracheae, painting spirals of cold across each breast.

'The second bowl brimmed with raspberries. The third, newly whipped cream, which he spooned onto corners of her elbows, the hollows above her ice-chilled clavicle, and the back of her neck. The raspberries fit her nipples like knitted hats, their flesh reminiscent of her own but newer, sweeter. He impaled a fat one on the end of his index finger and placed it against her lips. She took the finger in her mouth to the first knuckle, and drew upwards slowly, leaving it bare. The raspberry burst, the juice sweetened the powerful liquor of vanilla extract on his fingertips.

'He paused again. When the last, and ice-cold, spoon touched her sex, she cried out and sat bolt upright. He pushed her back down, insistently. She covered her face with her hands, unable to watch as he spooned sorbet onto the hillock below her navel, turning it into a snow-capped peak. Shivering she tried to hold still, unsure if she could endure more cold. Then suddenly, Antonio's tongue, now hot and furious, punctured the ice, furrowing, driving back the clear cold.

'Her legs parted. Her body's feast was chilled and glazed. Antonio found each cold drop.

'The boy had been well taught. A diligent apprentice, he knew: it's the contrast of flavours that tantalises. The body's proteins, all sour and salt and whey – bitter even in places. What was missing in that meal was sweetness. Sugar to match the musk and salt.

'Carolyn cupped his face, brought it to hers and kissed, tasting the tang of her sex, lemon, sugar, the salt of her last swim. She wrapped her arms around his neck, her legs around his hips, and he lifted her from the table, slick and shivering against him. They paused and swayed in the centre of the room, exchanging temperature, savouring the pressure of one nakedness against another. She slid down him slowly, landing on her knees, and clasped his wrists, shackling him.

'And Carolyn discovered: at first, men taste of their work. What is on their hands ends up in their pants. Mechanics, of car grease and gasoline. Carpenters, of sawdust or varnish. Fishermen, of diesel and bait. All of which gives way to their real taste – earthy, salty, sour – the sap you summon from manhood by stroking. And the baker tasted of flour, vanilla, lemon, coconut oil, cinnamon, sugar. The crotch bakes its scent into the air around it.

'He broke her grasp on his wrists, pulled her to her feet, placed his mouth hard against hers, theirs tongue stirring, their flavours mingling, while they tumbled to the floor. The soft nibbling, the tastings, the delicacies over. In sex, samplings only whet the appetite further, they never fill you up.

'She pushed him to the tiles, and put him between her thighs. Slowly, so slowly that he twitched, she lowered herself.

He pushed his torso upright and they embraced and rocked together. For a second, they might believe, they would spend their entire lives making love under tables heavy with ice cream and marzipan.

'She began to rock. He propped up on his elbows, so they can both watch their coupling. Both young enough that it was still novelty for a part of one person to disappear inside another, and reappear, and disappear. Her rise and fall increased in arc and speed, until he stopped her, made her pause at the top of his organ. She overcame him, gyrating in short fierce strokes. He sat up, their torsos wrapped each other. His mouth on hers and her mouth on his, her tongue inside him, and his organ inside her. Until she cried out and he cried out and he lifted her again, and their syrup spilled between them. And she collapsed against him, and in that embrace, they slid to the floor.'

Beneath the plush red headboard, Antonio Ferrara II felt himself rising. He walked his fingers from Zsuzsa's crotch to her nose, bringing the scent of their mixings to her in a small dab of perfume, before returning to gather more. She curled towards pleasure. The closest piece of flesh was his arm and she bit into his bicep, tugging gently at his skin. His underarms smelled of cinnamon and clove, the skin ever so slightly sour, like unsweetened kefir. Beneath his skin, his muscles were deliciously marbled. She bit hard enough to leave marks. He pulled her towards him.

Another climax. Another cigarette.

'More?' she asked.

'More.'

'Perhaps it was too warm to stay that way, so they lay next to each other, staring up at the stucco ceiling, the pads of their index fingers touching, occasionally pushing against each other. Their abdomens daubed with paste – the flour from the worktop, their sauces, their sweat.

'Perhaps they coupled again. And again. Until the entire floor was sticky, until the storeroom was carnage, and their bodies ran out of ingredients.

'Just before dawn, they stood at the sink, washing each other. He helped her dress. And, for the last time, he stroked the side of her face, touched her hair.'

'And?'

'And nothing. She got back on the boat. Forever after, she would associate sweets with sex. She would become stunningly voluptuous, taking on the likeness of his dough statues, just as they would take on the likeness of her.

'And that is the end of our story, and that is the end of our night, Dragam. One more cigarette and you must go.'

It was very late when Antonio Ferrera II left the house of his mistress. Without thinking, he walked three blocks westward and two blocks southward and found himself looking at the still masts of the harbour. His hands smelt of the scent of sex and marzipan. The night was still pleasantly sticky.

The pleasantness was interrupted by a draft of cigarette smoke. He looked about. It was still too early for his son to be at work.

As he turned towards his shop, a jolt moved through him. A faint luminance glowed in the window, backlighting the figure of a woman. A figure so well proportioned that his twice-spent arousal returned. He strode to the storefront and put his hands and face against the glass. There, rendered in pastry dough, was a narrow waist, a stunningly curved hip, and three fine hair-lines below her bellybutton.

He put a hand to his heart.

Light spilled from the door to the storeroom, which was slightly ajar. From the back of the shop, he heard the voice of his son, murmuring, '*Bravo. Bravo.*'

Harsingar

AMITAVA KUMAR

N O ONE WHO was even half-literate in Hindi in the early seventies would have missed the short-story 'Bungalow Number 43'. The story's author was Satyadev. His real name was Akhilesh Jha and he was the son of a woman, now dead, who had once been a famous dancer in Patna.

Satyadev would have been in his thirties when I first became aware of him. He lived on our street. His house was next to ours; it was a modest yellow house with a small mango tree in the garden.

Next door to Satyadev, further away from us, was my friend Ali's house. Ali was only a year older than me but he had experienced the world. If you watched a Hindi film with him, he could predict how the film would end. He was also good at football and had already smoked his first cigarette. He was ten years old.

One day, when coming back from school, Ali told me that his maternal uncle had given him a set of new Montana table-tennis balls. If I came over at four, he would show them to me. And then we would walk over to the Railway Club and see if we could get to play on the table there.

I didn't find Ali in his room and I went to the kitchen to see if he was still eating. Ali's family, just like ours, ate in the kitchen or in the small screened room that connected the kitchen to the living room. But the kitchen was empty.

I then looked in the bedroom and thought that maybe I had made a mistake and come to the wrong house. Satyadev was standing near the window. The room was dark but sunlight shone on the curls on his head. He was wearing a cream-colored kurta and his legs were bare like a wrestler's. Satyadev was pushing – plunging was a word I would acquire later – against someone whose head was thrown back. She had a hand on the windowsill. I saw now that it was Mrs Rizwi, Ali's mother, in her own bedroom. Her eyes were on the ceiling or maybe even the sky outside. Her lovely mouth, which I had often seen stained with paan, was open in pleasure or pain, I couldn't tell. I dropped the curtain before I could see any more.

'Bungalow Number 43,' in case you haven't read the story, is about a young man who accidentally shoots his lover after they have had sex for the first time on his father's bed. The story is tender about sex, and brutal about its aftermath. I read the story in my late teens and never forgot it. I had found it shocking and it was only later that I saw it as a story not about sex but about death.

Satyadev's father was a Deputy Superintendent of Police. He had shot himself in his bedroom. My mother revealed this to me. Satyadev's father suspected that his wife was having an affair with a music director. My mother also mentioned that there is one detail in 'Bungalow Number 43' that is drawn from real life. The young woman in the story, a dancer, wears harsingar flowers in her hair. That is exactly how Satyadev's mother used to adorn her hair.

There's one thing I forgot to mention. Satyadev's house, though a small one, had a blue plaque on the gatepost. The plaque said 'Harsingar' in Hindi.

People in Patna say that Satyadev's mother had once performed in front of Pandit Nehru. But the family was never well-off and after the father's death they fell in status. For several years, Satyadev had earned his living by providing tuition.

Boys and girls who wanted to do well in their last high-school exams came to his house in groups of three or four each evening. They left just as dusk was gathering. I often watched them from my window. Ali would sometimes join me and we shared remarks about each girl as she left the house.

These girls, just a few years older than us, laughing and joking with their friends, appeared very desirable to the two of us. They often arrived alone or in pairs and waited under the mango tree for their other friends to show up. To our eyes, they were like beautiful birds and we, young as we were, wanted to hold them in our hands.

One evening, when we were sitting beside my window, Ali said that Satyadev was sleeping with one of the girls he was tutoring. I felt a stab of jealousy. Ali's mother had brought over some sewai one night and found Satyadev in his lungi and the girl, her hair loose, sitting on the tiny sofa next to him. He had his hand on her thigh.

That night after dinner, I went closer to Satyadev's house. The curtain, orange in colour and lit from the inside, covered only half of the bedroom window. There was a faint breeze and the curtain stirred but revealed nothing. I was near enough to hear the radio playing inside but it was impossible to know if there was anyone at home.

❦

In a year, my mother had said, I would be Satyadev's student too. She wanted me to get admitted into a good college. I was struggling in most subjects and, to be quite honest, I was distracted by the changes in my own body. Women occupied all my waking hours.

I'd open my eyes and my gaze would rest on Zeenat Aman looking into the distance while the artificial rain in the studio raked her partially-clothed breasts. This was a short-lived idyll. My mother tore down the poster that I had bought for eighty rupees, a small fortune.

Ali gave me a sympathetic ear. He had a sharp eye for the female form. But he was busy. Not with classes, where he excelled, but his extra-curriculars. He had stopped playing football, although he still competed in races, running the mile quicker than anyone else in the state. More of his time, however, was taken by his work on the stage. He was an actor. My mother said that Ali was a natural. I told her that he wanted to write plays. That was his real ambition. She said that he was so under-stated, and yet expressive, he should act in films.

I didn't want Ali to join films. He was my friend and I admired him but I didn't want him to be the one who was disrobing Zeenat Aman. When I said this to him, Ali laughed. Zeenie Baby is not for me, he said. He wanted Rekha. Rekha knew how to move her hips. She wouldn't just lie there in bed, he speculated. Then he brought his fingers to his lips and blew over them. Hot stuff, he said, and stroked his young beard.

Later that year, Ali acted in a play based on a Manto story. Satyadev had done the adaptation. Ali played a young man named Randhir who makes love to a working-class woman taking shelter from the monsoon in his apartment building. This was my Zeenat Aman fantasy coming alive on stage! Randhir wants the girl drenched with rain to change into dry clothes. When the knot on her blouse doesn't open, he tries to help and brushes her naked breasts. All of this was partially hidden from the audience but we were free to imagine as we listened to the voice-over narrate Manto's lines.

Not till some days had passed did I make another discovery about the play. For some reason, Ali had kept it a secret from me that the young woman whose blouse he was fumbling with was the same girl that we had known about for two years. She was the one that Satyadev had been sleeping with – the young woman that Ali's mother had first told us about. When I learned this fact, I wondered about Ali's silence. I found it strange.

And in my mind, as I continued to wonder about it, I heard the voice-over in the play I had watched. The director had chosen a woman's voice. In the silence of the auditorium, Manto's phrases floated in the air while Ali and Medha, for that was the tall dusky girl's name, moved like snakes in a mating dance. 'Her breasts had the pliancy, the moist roughness, and the cooling warmth of vessels that have just come off the potter's wheel.'

Two more years passed. I was now a student at Patna College. Eight months earlier, Ali left for Delhi to join the National School of Drama. My mother, too, had received an invitation from an institute in Shimla to take the position of a lecturer there but she was uncertain. This was largely because of me, and what she saw as my lack of direction. In the meantime, she had bought me a Bajaj scooter although I had wanted a motorbike instead. Life wasn't ideal but a new cinema hall had opened near us and I hoped to go there sometime with one of the girls from my college.

On a warm evening in March, I took Satyadev to Rabindra Bhawan for an awards ceremony. He was to receive the Premchand Puruskar for his new novel, *Platform*. A family arrives at the Patna railway station from a village in Siwan; they have brought an infant for medical treatment at the hospital. When the child dies, they come back to the railway station and never leave. The father has a broken leg and becomes a beggar; at first the surviving kids join him and then the older one becomes a pickpocket. The novel ended with the police making a list of the meager items in a red suitcase seized from the family on the platform.

Satyadev was dressed carefully. Silk kurta, burgundy shawl folded on one shoulder, the ringlets on his head dark and shiny. The Chief Justice, acting as the Interim Governor, gave him the award. A scroll and a check for thirty thousand rupees.

Satyadev didn't eat any of the food offered to him. He was presenting an ascetic self to the world. Lots of bowing with folded hands and smiles. After an hour, he gestured with his eyes and a small sweeping movement of the head that we could leave. For my new scooter, he used a term from the Ramayana for a mythical vehicle of flight. He wasn't mocking me. He only wanted to make me feel better. Which put us on par because I wanted to do the same to him.

I didn't mention Ali. Medha had left Satyadev, she had fallen in love with Ali. It surprised some of us but only because Medha was a few years older than Ali and everyone in Patna reacted as if there was something naturally illicit in this relationship.

A few people even tried to give the whole affair a communal tinge. All this gossiping was useless anyway because Medha had left Patna and was living in Delhi with Ali.

I had known about their relationship a little before it became public knowledge. It was raining one afternoon when Ali came to our door. Medha was with him. Ali asked if I could give them tea. I hurried to the kitchen, happy that I'd get a chance to talk to Medha who was indeed very pretty. Ali must have known my mother would be at work. He came to me in the kitchen and said that there was an important matter he wanted to discuss with Medha. Could I leave them alone for half an hour?

I took my umbrella. When I returned, both Ali and Medha thanked me politely and then left abruptly. That evening, Ali and I met again. There were puddles on the ground and we just stood at the gate, talking. Ali was secretive, or maybe just shy, and all he said was that he had never before made love to Medha while her clothes were wet from the rain. Today he had a chance to do what he had so often pretended to be doing on stage.

I was titillated and wanted to get more details. Instead, I asked about his doing this so close to Satyadev's house. Ali laughed. He said, Medha wanted to do it.

Motorcycles and cars, also a few rickshaws and men on bicycles, passed us while we stood at the gate. Ali was looking away from me in the dark and he began talking to me as if I was back in seventh class and he was entertaining me with stories about sex. Medha likes doing it everywhere, he said. She loves me, I know that, but there is also something more. Medha clings to me through the night and in the morning her mouth is everywhere. She has a hunger I have never experienced in anyone else. If she had her way, I think she'd want me to fuck her on top of a speeding train.

❧

So on that night when Satyadev received his award, I wanted to spare him any news of Ali. Ali had told me that Medha's body smelled like the earth after the first rain. Were those his own words or Manto's? I didn't know. The truth was that Ali didn't need Manto. A review in *The Statesman* had praised his playwriting and acting in 'Chai Factory.' This was his new play about college students who meet in a café to discuss a professor's arrest following allegations of sexual abuse.

On our way back on the scooter, Satyadev shouted in my ear that he was hungry. He said, I have received thirty thousand rupees today and would like to spend a small portion of it on Chinese food.

We brought the food in white polythene packets back to Satyadev's house. The spicy chicken chow mein and chilli chicken we washed down with glasses of Old Monk rum. The drink went to my head. I said to Satyadev, Why don't you get married? I saw that you had many female admirers tonight.

His smile was strained. He said, Yes, I probably should get married, now that the government has given me so much money.

From somewhere the thought came that Ali had used me and forgotten me. He hadn't bothered to write or call – the old complaint of those who are left behind – while Satyadev had not abandoned his roots. Even Ali's mother still liked him, and visited his home sometimes to deliver snacks. I suddenly said, I'm sorry about what happened with Ali. You have reason to—

Satyadev looked at me and I knew I ought to stop.

He was silent for a while. He didn't take deep gulps of rum from his glass, or sigh dramatically, or make bitter, sarcastic remarks. He stayed so still that I thought that he had slipped into a deep, paralysing sorrow. But, in reality, Satyadev was utterly serene. This was evident when he began to speak. He put his case most simply.

This award I got today, he said, I didn't hear about till only five days ago because I wasn't here. I was in Delhi. I had gone there to watch 'Chai Factory.' I had been curious. The old professor in the play wasn't me. But Ali had given him some of my habits. He is a good observer, and his portrait was convincing. The role he had written for Medha was more revealing. I was once her lover, remember? But what he had her say on stage, what he had her do, was extraordinary. It was as if I was discovering her in a new way. No, it was as if she was discovering herself as an individual with independent desires. It was a magical experience. He is a true artist. His private life is not my business and, as far as I'm concerned, to even ask what type of person he is in everyday life is a complete waste of time.

All of this happened a long time ago. Several decades have passed, time building walls and then breaking them down. But all of this came back to me tonight when I got a note from a writer friend of mine telling me that he had broken up with his girlfriend. I felt sorry for him but his girlfriend interested me. I have admired her almost equally for her beauty and for her ability to produce prose of startling truthfulness.

I called up my friend to sympathise; my loyalty to him prevented me from calling his girlfriend instead. His note had flung me into an abyss. The woman I had long coveted, whose cheekbones and mouth had fascinated me during so many conversations, was now free. But, as I said, I called my friend first.

He answered the phone immediately and then proceeded to tell me that he had ended the relationship because after he had made clear that he wasn't going to get married his girlfriend had hooked up with some fellow she had met on Facebook. They had spent a weekend in a hotel in Rajasthan, as my friend put it, 'fucking the brains out of each other'.

That phrase sent a jolt through me. Why did she not call me instead? I would have devoted so much attention to her limbs, her lips, her small breasts. I had loved her for years. My friend was certain that she was mad but I yearned for her, and had done so for years, in a way that no stranger found on Facebook possibly could. The kind of candour she used to bring to her statements – I'd have wanted to do the same for a night. Before I fuck you I want to lick you. Let me touch you this way, and this way. Now turn this way, no this way, and open your mouth please, and spread your legs. Get on your knees.

I was consumed with these thoughts for a while but even before I had poured a measure of rum out for myself I remembered Satyadev. I've never been able to forget what he had said about what it means to be an artist. And that is why instead of getting completely drunk I sat down and wrote this account taking me back to a blank afternoon when I first encountered sex.

Naked Cleaning Lady

JAISHREE MISRA

SHE SPOTTED THE advertisement after buying the papers at the newsagents down Walworth Road. It was a handwritten note, fluttering between a photocopied picture of a lost cat and a yellow post-it describing a 1996 Kenwood mixie that was for sale. Pretending to be looking at the glossy magazines on the stand below, Saira read the words again, feeling a small quickening of her heartbeat.

LOOKING FOR A LADY (35-55) TO CLEAN THE HOME
OF A SINGLE, ELDERLY GENT.
HOOVERING, DISHES, LAUNDRY, NO COOKING.
WILLING TO PAY £25 PER HOUR PROVIDED THE LADY
IS PREPARED TO CARRY OUT SAID TASKS WITHOUT THE
ENCUMBRANCE OF HAVING CLOTHES ON.
NO ULTERIOR MOTIVE. PERSONAL SAFETY & TOTAL
COURTESY GUARANTEED.
IF INTERESTED, PLEASE CALL 07817113224.

£25 an hour! She may well have whipped out her mobile phone and called straightaway from the shop, or perhaps from the street as a concession, but this was surely not going to be an *uncomplicated* conversation so it would need to wait. Yes, of

course, she should worry about the no-encumbrance-of-clothing
bit. It was definitely weird but something about the old-fashioned
language did make the single-elderly-gent bit sound genuine.
What was the worst a single elderly gent could do anyway?
Pounce on her, perhaps, but years of kick-boxing sessions back
in high-school had given her some very useful muscle groups.
She ought to be cautious really but the advert didn't sound
like someone looking for a hooker: there were surely plenty of
other places one could go to for that kind of thing rather than
the notice-board of a local shop. It was decided. She would
call and apply for the job. If one could call it that. Given how
few proper jobs were showing up in the local paper, there was
something distinctly godsend-ish about spotting this one. Her
money situation was getting close to the edge and the naked
bit was almost an irrelevance, seeing how little Saira thought
about her body at most times.

Memorising numbers wasn't a problem as Saira knew from
her distant aborted accountancy career but, to be on the safe
side, she pulled out a pen and jotted the phone number down
on her palm. She did not want to risk forgetting it by the time
she got back home, seeing that she still had the vegetables to buy,
and two light-bulbs for the faux-chandelier in the hallway that
had lain dark, somewhat appropriately, ever since Tim had left.

Three weeks. Amazingly, it was three weeks already, although
it felt like a lot less. 'Like yesterday' as the cliché went. Why did
everyone spout clichés at a time of crisis, Saira wondered. But
she would not be surprised if Tim's departure would, in fact,
always seem like yesterday, even many, many years down the
line. Perhaps decades on even. Surely such rawness of pain and
confusion didn't magically heal over time, much as people kept

assuring her of that other cliché. More than anything else, what she deserved to be most haunted by was her own stupidity actually. The kind of unseeing idiocy that had kept her so completely unaware of Tim's two-year long affair with his colleague. Not to mention the baby they were now going to have together. Our baby's due in July, he had said, not without a hint of fatherly pride. Which was why he had to leave immediately. With barely a goodbye or apology or a decent winding-up period. And, no, there certainly wasn't any point in trying to patch things up or repairing their marriage nor even making another attempt at having a baby of their own. It was much too late for all that now. And that was before even taking into consideration Saira's body-clock that, as far as she knew, was about to stop ticking at any minute. Whatever happened if a body-clock stopped ticking halfway through making a baby, Saira had sometimes wondered. But there was no chance of that happening now anyway. She wasn't really the best judge of bodily matters as focusing too much on one's physical self had always seemed like a vaguely narcissistic kind of thing to do.

Arriving at East Street Market, Saira hovered at the fringes of the vegetable stall, trying not to push her way past two burly West Indian women who were filling their trolley basket with fat tubers of tapioca and yellow plaintains oozing with sweetness. What rambunctious family feast were they preparing for? Saira imagined them presiding over a heaving table surrounded by laughing children. It was only ten a.m. but the market was already thrumming with shoppers, despite the thin icy drizzle that had been falling all morning. The hawker standing outside the Pakistani fish stall was belting out his version of the 'One pound fish' jingle in a heavy Pakistani accent. He smiled

encouragingly at Saira who occasionally bought frozen packs
of Bangladeshi prawns from his store but she ducked his gaze
under the hood of her anorak. In truth, she had no desire for
fish, fowl or vegetable – food had taken on the taste of ashes
and, these days, seemed to pass right through her system with
little regard for either digestion or nutrition. But having found
the fridge almost completely bare this morning, save for a
mouldy piece of cheese and half a pint of soured milk, Saira had
finally gathered herself up and decided to brave the world. If
for nothing else, she needed to lay her eyes upon the normality
of other people going about their business. Else there was every
chance she would go mad or starve to death and what would
be the good of that?

Saira reached out for a shiny purple aubergine, imagining
the spicy, smoky bhartha she could expertly convert it into, and
was surprised at the sudden flicker of appetite at the thought
of her favourite dish. Spotting the phone number half-hidden
under the plump aubergine cupped in her hand, she thought
about the 'gent' who had placed the ad in the shop. Who could
he be and why the kink? Was it a kink? Or was he, like her, a
lonely soul, merely trying to eke a bit of excitement out of life?
While Sarah could understand trying to achieve a modicum of
joy via an aubergine, it mystified her that happiness could also be
had by looking at someone's naked parts. Men were mystifying
creatures at the best of times.

It suddenly occurred to Saira that there may be other takers
for the job. After all, £25 an hour was not to be sneezed at
in the midst of a double recession. Particularly when Tim had,
unbeknown to her, virtually cleaned out their joint account in
the weeks before leaving. She had better hurry home and make

that phone call right away. The light-bulbs could wait another day or two as Saira now knew that a hallway plunged in darkness was really not the end of the world; having no money and no self-worth was.

Trotting down the road, she stumbled into her doorway, slammed the door behind her, pulled out her mobile phone and pressed the numbers on its keypad, reading them off her palm in the thin light that was filtering down from the fanlight.

He opened the door and looked at the slight Asian woman standing on his doorstep.

'Saira,' she said, with a question mark inflexing the latter syllable.

He had mis-heard it as 'Sarah' in their phone conversation and her accent had been too neutral to tell that she was Asian. But never mind. She seemed presentable enough, slim and neat, long black hair tied back in a ponytail. He ushered her into the hallway and took her jacket, shaking it free of raindrops before hanging it close to the radiator to dry. Yes, she had much more the kind of figure he'd had in mind compared to the enormous Jamaican lady he had seen at three p.m. and the scrawny white girl who had followed at four. Heroin-addict, he was sure, which went completely against all his principles. It had not been a successful search at all so far.

Frank followed Saira into the living room and waved at the armchair next to the window.

'Tea?' he asked and she nodded.

When he returned with the tea-tray to the living room, he saw Saira looking at the photographs on his mantelpiece.

'I suppose you've pieced together a bit about me then,' he said, handing her the mug and putting the plate of cookies on the table as she shook her head at them. 'I promise they're real pictures and not a made-up collection designed to hoodwink you.'

She had a nice smile that came on unexpectedly. The photographs had helped take some of her nervousness away he could see. 'Well, that one's definitely not made up. It's clearly you,' she said, pointing at the picture that was taken on the day of his retirement from the bank, surrounded by colleagues holding a large boxed gift. He was at least ten years younger in that photo but recognisably the same person. Saira moved sideways, this time to peer at the old sepia picture of him and Joan on their wedding day. She looked enquiringly at him over the rim of her mug.

'Oh, yes, that's me too. Except, taken about a hundred years ago.'

She glanced at the photo again, taking her right hand off the mug to run a finger gently over the silver frame. 'She's gone, I take it,' she said, surprising him with her directness.

'Gone, yes,' Frank replied, 'Not long now. Last month, in fact. After a terribly long battle with cancer.'

'Oh, I'm so sorry.'

'Well, at least it's over now.' He cleared his throat. Even after nearly half a dozen interviews, it wasn't easy to explain. But he was going to have to, in fact for the fifth time today. 'Which is what this is all about, I suppose you've guessed. Call it trying to fight loneliness. Or some kind of weird self-therapy. But, for a number of reasons, I felt having someone around the house a couple of times a week would be nice. The least complicated way was to get a cleaner.' He cleared his throat again. 'And I hope you don't think it *kinky* or anything but the naked thing is really just something that will remind me of Joan, my wife, who always did the cleaning naked.' He stopped, as though waiting for a reaction and then, thinking the better of it, ploughed on in a hurry. 'It started off with Joan saying she didn't want to spoil her clothes. She was a bit pernickety about clothes and such things, you see. But then she started enjoying her nakedness and it became a bit of fun. It was just one of those quirks that even our daughter never knew about. She's in America now – my daughter, of course, not Joanie...'

Saira cut in, probably sensing that he was now rambling out of nervousness. 'You don't need to explain all this to me, Mr...?'

'Frank Gunner. Frank, just call me Frank.'

'Well, Frank, you are paying quite well so you don't need to explain too much really. I suppose I just need a bit of reassurance that it won't lead to anything else.'

'Oh, absolutely!' Frank decided to take the plunge and make his final confession, awkward as it was. 'It couldn't lead to anything else anyway, my dear, as I've been impotent for years. Something about Joan's illness and pain but everything inside me seemed to dry up as well in those years. I may look the spitting image of a porn star but I promise I haven't had an erection in years. You're perfectly safe on that count.'

Saira laughed and Frank made a quick decision. 'So when can you start?' he asked.

❦

The following afternoon, Frank opened the door to Saira, noticing that she was dressed more carefully than the last time. Her jacket looked newer, and underneath was a belted white top over a pair of well-fitted navy jeans. In her ears were a pair of dangling pearls and she had left her hair open today, brushed out and shiny as it ran over her shoulders in dark waves.

As had been agreed, he escorted her into the living room where the drapes had been drawn tightly shut. The only light came from three pedestal lamps that cast pools of mellow light over the carpet and sofas.

Frank settled himself into an armchair and picked up a newspaper, pretending to read, while, at the other end of the room, Saira started to take her clothes off. In one swift movement, she pulled her top off, revealing a pert pair of breasts cradled in a lacy mauve bra. Frank saw how her hint of cleavage became darker and deeper as she squeezed her arms before her to tackle the buttons of her jeans. Her long hair fell curtain-like over her face as she kicked off her shoes and bent over to pull off first one leg of her jeans and then the other. Saira shot a look at Frank while folding her clothes to hang them on the back of an armchair. Their gaze met for a brief second before Frank hurriedly buried his face back into his newspaper. She was a lot prettier, her body far younger than he had imagined on meeting her yesterday. He hadn't asked her much about herself but had gathered from her conversation that she had no husband and no children, which probably explained her taut brown stomach and firm breasts. Yesterday, he had assumed she was about fifty years old, going by an air of disappointment that hung around her. Now that she looked more cheerful, and had revealed such a nicely muscled body, he wasn't so sure.

'These as well?' she asked, gesturing to her undergarments. Frank nodded, not daring to speak lest his voice should emerge in a squeak. Seemingly unperturbed, Saira expertly unhooked her bra and flung it over her clothes before steadying herself against the back of the armchair to peel off her knickers. Now she stood stark naked in the middle of Frank's living room, suddenly cutting a taller and more regal figure than she was when fully clothed. Despite the pretence of the newspaper, Frank gazed open-mouthed at Saira's brown breasts, capped by twin chocolate aureolae, her pubic hair a soft dark triangle disappearing between her thighs.

'Hoover?' she asked.

'Ah, yes, of course, of course,' Frank said, scrambling out of his chair and disappearing into the kitchen. He turned to find that Saira had followed him and was standing barefoot on the linoleum. 'Your feet, you'll catch cold, oh my goodness, the blinds, I forgot,' Frank said, lunging for the kitchen window and yanking the wooden blinds down with a crash.

Saira took the hoover from Frank and bent over to pull the plug cord out. Suddenly Frank was treated to the sight of Saira's up-ended bare bottom as she bowed to push the cord into the nearest electric socket. Fearing he might pass out, he mumbled an excuse before slipping back into the living room.

Frank sank into his armchair and closed his eyes, trying – as he had done so many times these past few weeks – to try and remember Joan's pretty little body before it had become so ravaged by her illness. The very first time she had carried out her naked cleaning experiment, she had appeared at the kitchen door, starkers, except for a pair of bright red pumps and lipstick. It had been the most amazing thing that Frank had ever experienced and had led to magnificent, electrifying sex right there on the carpet. Frank looked at the fake deerskin rug that lay before the now unlit fireplace, remembering Joan's body lying spread-eagled and wanton while he ran his tongue over every inch of her skin: her breasts, her belly-button, her rose-pink nipples turned to gold by the fire in the grating.

Of course, even those trysts had gradually evolved into a faintly mischievous and playful titillatory game that, on especially hectic cleaning days, did not even culminate in sex. But that was what forty years of marriage did, Frank knew, turning the wildly exhilarating into something far more comforting and lulling. He hoped he had not made a mistake in embarking on this rather mad-cap experiment now, thought up merely to cheer himself a bit. After all, Joan had explicitly told him to get some money out of their joint savings account to do something he would enjoy after she had died. 'Go on a cruise, Frank,' she had urged, 'meet some nice women. Somewhere, anywhere, sunny and bright. Whatever you do, I don't want to think of you moping all by yourself here in this house.'

Well, he certainly wasn't alone in the house now but this was probably not what Joanie had meant. And that Asian girl now hoovering his kitchen seemed like a decent sort too. Surely she would have never once considered doing her (or anyone else's) cleaning in the buff. She did have a rather nice body, though. Well, sexier than Frank had initially thought. Especially when she had bent over and stuck her bottom out at him. Oh dear, inducing a stroke at his age would not be wise.

Frank tried to immerse himself in his newspaper again, trying to soothe his nerves with the humming sound of the hoover in the kitchen. All he had to do now was imagine it was yesterday once more, with Joan – lovely, sweet Joan – back in their kitchen and just about to come into the living room to jiggle her boobies suggestively at him as she ran her feather duster around all her old artefacts, him included...

Instead, Saira appeared at the door, glowing golden in the soft light as she hoovered the floor vigorously, working up a sweat. In a few stolen glances, Frank saw her breasts swing from side to side and, as she turned, the muscles in her haunches tensed almost animal-like, her toes squeezing tightly into the pile of the carpet. Her back was long and lithe with a pleasant dip in the middle which culminated in that marvellous dark crack separating the globes of her buttocks...

In half an hour, Saira had finished the hoovering. Frank's was only a small two-bedroom bungalow, not much bigger than her own flat, but she had developed a surprising head of steam, having tackled her work with the kind of energy she had not been able to muster up these past few weeks. Being naked had been surprisingly liberating too, once she had gotten over the awkwardness of Frank's bulging blue gaze. The poor old boy was clearly not a standard pervert, more embarrassed than aroused by the whole business but who was she to question it? He was paying well, she needed the money and, if she were honest, Frank's admiring glances had been like salve on that terribly painful wound called Tim. She could not even remember when Tim had last wanted to see her naked.

Saira put the hoover away behind the kitchen door and squatted to empty the washing machine. Holding the damp clothes against her heated body as she stood up gave her a momentary frisson. Her skin had forgotten what touch felt like, she realised. Not that she had stopped to consider it with any concern before this but no one had touched her body in months. No stroking, no massaging, no nibbling, none of the things a woman's skin needed in order to come awake and bloom like a flower. Now, almost in defiance of that deprivation, Saira stood in Frank's kitchen and used a freshly-washed hand towel to slowly wipe down her perspiring body. She massaged her breasts, moving the towel into the crease below before sliding it slowly downwards over her stomach and between her legs. She emitted a small moan as she felt a thrill pass through her groin. Perhaps Frank was watching through the kitchen door but it did not matter. In fact, if he was also gaining pleasure from it, Saira was glad, very glad.

After Saira had got dressed and left, tucking her money into her handbag with a wide grin on her face, Frank came back into the living room and sank into his armchair, exhausted. He had not realised how draining the experience would be. Having a naked woman around the house who was not his Joanie had been a completely different experience to anything he had known before. Saira, who had seemed so mousy and uncertain on their first meeting, had been strangely transformed by her nakedness, strutting about the house like a barefoot Amazon, carrying hoovers and ironing boards around as though they weighed nothing at all. Besides, her slight body had seemed to take on a height and shape that had not existed before she had so confidently taken all her clothes off. Perhaps it was because she had slipped so effortlessly into the role – whatever vestiges of shame Frank had felt slipped away. He leant his head back on the cushion, remembering the way in which Saira had wiped herself down after finishing the hoovering, probably unaware that he was watching from afar. He saw again the slow sensual movements as she had pleasured herself, delighting in her own attractiveness, loving every niche and curve of her beautiful body. And then Frank felt a stirring that he had not experienced in a long, long time. Not since Joan had fallen ill and they had both sunk into the depths of despair together. He looked down at his groin and there it was – sticking up stiff against his corduroy trousers – a gloriously huge erection.

The Degradation of Erasmo S.

CYRUS MISTRY

ONE MORNING AT breakfast while eating toast and sipping coffee, Erasmo Sequiera read through the entire newspaper holding it upside down. His sister Alberta was awestruck, but said nothing to bring the discrepancy to his notice. He seemed frighteningly absorbed. That was the first time Alberta noticed that her brother was showing some signs of strain.

He was forty-one, a tall thin man with a pencil-line moustache, big eyes, big ears, a weak chin that almost merged with his neck and an awkwardness that came from having excessively long limbs. In his younger days, he was considered quite dapper and a witty charmer. Always smartly dressed, his hair pomaded and slickly pushed back, he carried a large gold watch suspended by a shiny chain and withdrew it periodically from his waistcoat pocket to frown at through bushy, puckered eyebrows. This action of his had become so automatic that he would repeat it unthinkingly even in church on Sundays, during the priest's long and generally tedious sermons; much to the annoyance of Alberta, who would nudge him viciously to arrest this rudeness.

But time had taken its toll on Erasmo. His wardrobe had deteriorated and he had not the means to replenish it. His fine moustache had sprouted white hairs. The straight line of the parting in his hair, which he had methodically exacted for years, had become a meandering pathway through patches of baldness. And his watch, his beloved gold watch, which had belonged to his father before him, had smashed to bits when he was violently hurled out of a public bus which accelerated before he could find a foothold. He no longer indulged in the witticisms for which he was once famous, but spoke little, in a gruff, low voice.

In the mixed boys' and girls' school where he had taught for seven years, he was respected for his learning and feared for his fits of temper. He had a quaint manner of twirling a wooden pointer between his fingers as he lectured, rapping it demonstratively on the blackboard now and then; or sometimes, when angry, on the knuckles of incorrigible rowdies and dunces at whom he would splutter, 'Bloody bullocks! Asinine gogs!' But, generally speaking, the children weren't afraid of him. They knew of a soft streak in his heart and used it to their merry advantage.

Especially on days when some homework or composition had become due for checking, they would easily distract him with appeals for stories, jokes or songs. And though he grumbled, Erasmo would give in with an obvious pleasure. He would tell them tales from Greek mythology, from Grimm and Anderson, recite long verses of doggerel by Lewis Carroll or Edward Lear from memory. Or he would allow the children to come up front and tell their own stories or jokes in turn. Sometimes when the mood was on him and he was melancholy, Erasmo would even stride up to the passage door, shut it, and sing before a hushed classroom: songs in Konkani and Portuguese he had learnt from his father's servants on their ancient sprawling estate in rural Goa, years and years ago...

The truth was that though he performed his duties as a teacher meticulously, Erasmo's heart was not in his work anymore. He felt tired. Of late, strange feelings of disquiet and anxiety had stirred in him, which he hadn't been able to place his finger on. Strange dreams had disturbed his sleep. Recently, it was true, there had been too much bickering and politics in the staff room as well. A new headmistress had been appointed by the school, a crass shrill woman with the most enormous pointed breasts, who for some reason seemed to bear a grudge against him. Perhaps, he suspected, she resented the older staff their seniority, and wanted to replace them with a newer lot.

Still, nothing had changed so drastically in his life to account for the sudden silent distress that had crept up on Erasmo, leaving him empty, aching with an unnameable rancour. Its symptoms were evident to him. Standing before a class full of children in their starched white shorts and skirts, Erasmo's breathing sometimes became strenuous and difficult. When this happened he suffered memory lapses, his mind went blank, and he started sweating profusely. A nasty tic had made its appearance in the corner of his mouth, causing his lips to jerk involuntarily in a sidelong direction at rapid intervals, giving him the appearance of snarling viciously at nothing in particular. In the past, Erasmo had been fond of taking a drink or two, but only in the evenings, after dark. Now, in his troubled state, he broke this rule and even began to maintain a bottle in his school locker.

One evening after school was over and he had partaken of refreshments in the staff room, Erasmo sat in an empty classroom giving extra tuition to a backward child. The girl, who was only eight or nine years old, was very distracted as always, recalcitrant and unwilling to attend. She hated this extra hour of school, after all her friends had gone home, that had been enjoined upon her by her parents.

'Sir, let me go early today, no, please, sir? I got to go somewhere, sir...'

'Very well,' said Erasmo. 'But first we must do some dictation.'

'No, sir, please, sir, I'm so tired,' the child protested. Then cheekily, 'First you must sing me a song, sir.'

Erasmo growled and even raised his hand threateningly. Then instantly ashamed, he said, 'Okay, song first, then dictation. Yes?' He picked up the child, placed her on his knobby knees and rocked her 'horsey' fashion, while singing,

'This old man, he came one, he played knick-knack on my gun, knick-knack paddy-wag give a dog a bone, this old man came rolling home...'

The child clapped along, beaming with joy.

'This old man, he came two, he played knick-knack on my shoe...'

Before he had run through the verses, an awful thing happened. Mrs Billimoria, the headmistress, who happened to be passing down the corridor, heard the singing, the chuckling, the clapping, and stuck her head and her monstrous breasts in at the door. She froze at what she saw: long-limbed Erasmo slouching on a desktop, swinging his legs, bouncing the child to the rhythm of some nonsense verse she was anyway too old to be learning. In a sour, bitterly contemptuous voice, she exclaimed:

'So this is how we give tuitions! Really, Mr Sequiera!' Then she turned and stomped away.

Some devil chuckled in Erasmo's breast and, instead of ceasing his song immediately, as he should have, he changed his tune and sang louder than before:

'Where are you going, Billy-boy, Billy-boy? Where are you going, charming Billy? I am going to see my wife, she's the idol of my life,' his voice strained to crescendo, smarting the stung headmistress all the way to the end of the corridor, 'but she's a young thing and cannot leave her mother!' Erasmo hadn't felt so good in years. He gave the delighted child leave to go home.

Late next morning, Mrs Billimoria summoned Erasmo to her office while he was taking a class. He admonished the children to remain silent and went out.

In her office, the headmistress did not look up as he entered. While he stood before her desk waiting, she signed a letter, and handed it to him to read. It was a curt note stating that his services had been terminated on grounds of incompetence and misbehaviour with children. In short he was being asked to collect his dues and clear out. Erasmo was dumbstruck. A terrible rage was bubbling on his lips. He began to stutter, 'How... how...how can you...?' But no words came to him. Quietly he turned to go. The headmistress, however, could not resist a parting shot:

'We don't want any perverts here, Mr Sequiera,' she leered at him with a lascivious gleam in her eye. 'Nor any drunks either...'

That look she gave him and the words she spoke sank deep. His hair stood on end and he was shivering as he left her office. Just then, the booming silver chimes of the school bell announced the lunch break. Hundreds of young children began pouring out of their classrooms. He watched them in a daze, felt their smooth bodies brush against him, jostle him, disregard him as they stampeded down the stairs, arms flailing, skirts flying, spurred on by voracious appetites. In that instant, a sleeping demon awoke in Erasmo, ravenous and hungry for gratification, and he realised, with horror and amazement that for so many years it had never occurred to him how much he longed to fondle those soft young breasts and frail tender bodies, how insanely he desired those delicate buds.

Erasmo concealed the news of his dismissal from his sister Alberta for over a month. Alberta was eight years older than Erasmo. Quite as tall, but heavily built, she stooped a little from the weight of her anterior mounds of flesh; her protuberant rear bobbed in a fascinating rhythmic movement when she walked. She was a teacher too, but at the University, where she took courses in Chaucer and Middle English.

Erasmo had always been a little afraid of Alberta. Their mother, Rose, had died when he was only two. Their father, Gabriel, had died eight years later, pauperised, having drunk up most of his estate, fleeced of the rest of it by unscrupulous friends while in a state of intoxication; that is to say, during his waking hours. You could say it was Alberta who had raised him, inspired him to read, work hard, and follow the career she had chosen for herself, an academic one. Now the two of them lived together in a small flat in Byculla, which never received the direct light of the sun. Yevjaan, their old nanny from Goa, had come to Bombay to cook and clean for them. Their three rooms and kitchen were crowded with old furniture, cupboards, chairs, glass showcases filled with crockery, curios and mementoes.

Every morning, Erasmo would dress up as usual and leave the house in pretended haste, carrying with him a few files and notebooks. Alberta would leave shortly after, for the University. Erasmo would stop at the 154 bus stop for a few moments, look around, then walk briskly past it, round the neighbourhood block, across the road, cutting through three more lanes to arrive by a shortcut to the public gardens at the zoo. Once inside, having bought his entrance ticket, he would loosen his necktie and breathe more easily.

Erasmo was fascinated by the animals. He would saunter around the cages all morning, staring at the lions, the tiger, the monkeys and the elephants, making peculiar noises to attract their attention, trying to meet their eyes. He would carry a bag of peanuts with him to feed the animals, though this was against the rules. The park was scattered with others like him, people with little to do, loiterers and malingerers, unemployed men, office peons, schoolboys playing truant, vendors of popcorn and cold drinks, a few tourists, usually accompanied by children.

A little before noon he would leave the park and walk for ten minutes in an easterly direction to a neighbourhood country liquor bar called Polly's Place. Here Erasmo was afraid of meeting people who might recognise him. Occasionally, a local busybody would hail him, 'Professor! How is life?' and Erasmo would nod hastily and find a table as far away as possible. He would order a quarter of orange or mixed fruit and drink quietly, while having his 'lunch', which consisted of two boiled eggs, a chakli, and peanuts. When he had finished, he would walk back to the park, staggering a little in the afternoon sun.

Erasmo's mind was in a whirl. It did not even occur to him to try and look for another job. His age was against him and all his experience was naught now that he had been dismissed without any certificates to prove his past record. But more than that, even if he were to find another job, how would he ever face a class of children again? And teach? Erasmo's feverish obsessions gave him no rest. He was tossed and turned and flung about on a wild sea of fantasies, which, every day, grew more erotic and obscene and insistent. His waking hours were swamped in a deluge of desperate helplessness. At nights he slept heavily, a dreamless, dreary sleep, to wake each morning to this madness, this giddy desire that now controlled his life.

And his sense of shame was desperate too. It tore at his entrails and drove him to tears of self-condemnation. He was convinced of the truth of the headmistress's words, indeed they had made him aware of his sick condition. He was a pervert, a drunkard, a man without morals of any sort. Before he went to bed at night, he knelt on the floor and prayed. He begged for mercy, begged to be relieved, so that the next day should be a different one, with some reprieve from this unchanging hell. But even as he prayed, a suave mocking voice in his head ridiculed him – who was he praying to? – and laughed, certain in the knowledge of its bestial power. And the next day was like all the rest. He still went to mass on Sundays with his sister, but he did not go for confession. What could he confess to, when he was not even repentant, when that thing between his legs grew daily more demanding and ebullient?

At about four o'clock, Erasmo would rouse from his nap in the park and head homeward. On his way home, very often, he would stop at the 64 bus stop outside the Sacred Hearts' girls' school. At four-thirty, when school ended, shoals of young girls would stream out of the main gate and collect at the bus stop, giggling, teasing, playing practical jokes on one another, euphoric in their temporary freedom at end of day. It warmed Erasmo's heart just to hear their voices and their laughter. A few times he even boarded the bus with them, just to be in their midst, feel the pressure of their bodies against his as they crowded in.

When he returned home at five, Yevjaan would eye him suspiciously, because it was still much earlier than his normal hour of return – while he had been employed. He would go to his room and lie in bed restlessly, or pace about, waiting for his pupils to arrive. There were two girls who had continued to take private tuitions from him. They would come and spend an hour each in his room, one after the other.

Those were hours of exquisite torture for Erasmo. There was a study table with a white cloth laid over it, at which they would sit, the student to his right. He would pull his chair as close as possible to the girl so that his leg pressed against hers. Every time he reached out to turn a page or point to some line in the text, he would let his elbow or upper arm brush against her breasts. Every time he explained some point to her, he would place his hand in her lap and pat it, absent-mindedly. And every time she made some mistake in her exercises, he would pinch her inner thigh or squeeze her arm and shake her in gentle reprimand. For Erasmo, it was dizzying. His familiarities with his students became bolder and more adventurous day by day. But the girls seemed not to notice anything and gazed at him innocently as lambs.

One day Erasmo asked both his pupils to come together for a joint lesson. When they were seated on either side of him, he put his mouth to their ears and whispered to each in turn, a mathematical problem to solve. He warned both of them not to let the other see the solution they arrived at. As the girls bent over their books studiously, Erasmo felt elated and powerful, like a monarch. His desire had swollen to the point of pain, and today Erasmo could repress it no longer. Beneath the cover of the white tablecloth, moving his hands subtly, like a thief,

Erasmo released his erect member out of its constricting clothing and caressed it. One of the girls finished her calculations before the other. With great care, as if to prevent the other girl from spying her answer, Erasmo peered into the girl's book, pressing his cheek against hers, putting his arm around her slender body, allowing his fingers to touch her breast. Then the other girl finished and Erasmo looked into her book with the same tender curiosity. A white liquid splattered the wall only a foot away from their three pairs of knees, and Erasmo's body shuddered. Then, of course, that horrible feeling of shame and self-disgust, as the children packed their bags and left.

That evening, Alberta stormed into Erasmo's room without knocking. He was lying in bed staring at the ceiling. When he saw her face, he guessed instantly that somehow she had found out about his job.

'What has happened to you, Erasmo? Is this what we have come to? Did you think you could start keeping secrets from your own sister? And why do you lock your door to me so often nowadays?'

Erasmo could not bear to hear Alberta's high-pitched shrieky voice which rose many octaves when she was angry. It had a terrifying quality. He broke down and sobbed.

'They got rid of me, Alberta. They booted me out. How could I tell you, Alberta, how could I, after all you've done for me? And they are right. I am not fit to teach. I am an animal.'

'Bless me, Erasmo, what on earth are you talking about? What are you saying, you poor harried creature? I know what monsters these children can be. They have harassed you out of your wits. I told you always, be strict with them, be strict. But you are like a child yourself. Never mind. You can rest now for

some months. I am there to look after you…' And she caressed his
head and soothed him. But inwardly, she frowned and wondered
if Erasmo was losing his mind. Later that night, she made him
a bowl of hot Bovril soup which helped him to sleep soundly.

The next morning when Erasmo awoke, he felt as if a
weight had been lifted off his head. There were no more secrets
to keep, no more elaborate deceptions to concoct and defend.
He didn't care what anyone thought of him now. He was free.
Between desperation and the paralysis of shame, something new
was born in Erasmo, a reckless anger at the incarceration of his
pent desires. It pleased him, this new feeling of freedom and
defiance, it frothed in him like mirth. And he nurtured it secretly,
let it grow, like some devil child being reared in seclusion in a
witches' cove for that fateful day when he will be sprung upon
an unsuspecting world.

Now that Alberta knew, Erasmo no longer needed to spend
his day at the park. His behaviour became more and more
eccentric and unaccountable. Some days he stayed at home,
pacing about, exploring every nook and corner of their small flat,
opening every cupboard and showcase, looking through books
and papers, rummaging through his sister's clothes, examining her
ludicrously large underwear, peering into every vase and ashtray,
climbing up on a stool to reach inaccessible objects, pondering
over the junk that had accumulated through the years on the
tops of cupboards and underneath their beds. On other days,
he went out, taking long bus rides all over the city. He would
stare at the women on the roads, young women, old women,
middle-aged women, children – children he loved best of all –
pawing them indiscriminately every time an opportunity offered,
burying his face in their long hair in crowded situations, his

pulse racing, his brain consumed by an unhealthy prurience. On one occasion when he exceeded himself, a fat Sindhi lady gave him a resounding slap and abused him loudly in language that incited the public. Only his age and his frail appearance saved him from receiving a sound thrashing from a bunch of busybodies that soon gathered.

In the evening he returned home to his tuitions. His familiarities with the girls had increased to the point of their alarm, though they could not be certain and never complained. One day he asked them a riddle and told them to shut their eyes tightly and think of the answer and not open them till he said so. The riddle was: 'What is small and soft if you scorn it, but long and hard if you tickle it?' The girls sat with their eyes shut, their faces frowning with a fierce concentration as they searched their minds for the answer. In the end, they both said, 'Give up.' Erasmo asked them to open their eyes. And they saw the answer revealed to them in its full glory. He asked them to tickle it so that it could become even bigger. The girls took fright and began crying. They never came back. One of the parents wrote him a long abusive letter and threatened to contact the police. The father of the other girl paid Erasmo a visit in the evening two days later, while Alberta and Yevjaan had both gone out to the market. He took Erasmo by the collar and, without saying a word, began punching him on the face and in the stomach. Erasmo did not defend himself. At the end of the beating his face wore a bemused, dreamy expression. The man left behind his visiting card, saying, 'Get in touch if you want some more tel-maalish, you cock-sucking scoundrel!' Erasmo hardly heard him. His greatest regret was that both his pupils were gone.

When Alberta saw all the bruises and welts on Erasmo's face, it did not occur to her that they could be the result of a beating. Why should it? Who would want to beat a respectable elderly man like him? When she asked Erasmo how they had come about, he claimed ignorance. He blandly denied their existence. This made Alberta furious and she even held out a mirror to him and asked him to look for himself. Erasmo gazed placidly at his swollen face for a few minutes and persisted in saying that he saw nothing out of the ordinary, that his face had always looked like this.

Alberta was bewildered. As she lay awake in bed that night, a more insidious explanation flashed in her mind and she turned cold with fear. O don't be silly, she dismissed it immediately from her head; such things don't happen anymore, how ridiculous! But then... Alberta had heard too many tales of such cases in her childhood, of people possessed by malicious spirits and driven to self-debasement and destruction, whose bodies would erupt in inexplicable swellings and injuries they themselves could not perceive. And when she thought of Erasmo's recent obsessive behaviour, of his mysterious dismissal from school for some scandalous reason, of the chuckling she thought she heard from his room sometimes at dead of night, the uncanny welts, the stony rebellious distance he had acquired from her that saddened her no end, suddenly the explanation seemed no longer outlandish but more than plausible. Alberta crept out of her bed on tiptoe and, with hands shaking uncontrollably, latched her own bedroom door.

The year was drawing to an end. In a few days from now Christmas would be here again. The streets of Byculla, where so many Christians lived, were merry with the Yuletide spirit and innumerable Stars of Bethlehem lit up the streets at night. As his luck would have it, around this time, Erasmo received a visit from a distant cousin whom he hadn't seen since last Christmas.

Rufus, the cousin, had come not only to offer season's greetings but with a request for a very big favour which, he said, if acceded to would take a great load off his head. His daughter Theresa, he explained, was in her last year at school and badly in need of some immediate coaching, without which it was most likely that she would not be allowed to appear for her final exam. She had always been something of a duffer and could not afford to lose yet another year. Erasmo was delighted to be of assistance and generously waived the question of money when Rufus asked apologetically how much he would charge. Rufus suggested that they might start tuitions after the end of the festivities, if that was convenient but Erasmo insisted that they should start right away, just so that his daughter – what's her name? – had a head start.

Theresa was eighteen but looked much younger than that. She was small-built with straight long hair, wore thick powerful glasses and ill-fitting frocks that were too tight for her shoulders and made her hold them slightly bent. She seemed very timid and her face wore an expression of completely angelic innocence. Erasmo was amazed by her sweetness and beauty and resolved to teach her more attentively than he had his previous students. He was glad now that they were gone, so he could give all his time to Theresa. He saw her every day and kept her for two to three hours at a stretch.

In the company of Theresa, Erasmo regained all his youthful powers. He felt physically stronger and much more energetic, and to his own surprise, his wit and charm had begun to dazzle again. He turned its full force on Theresa. No doubt he spent a certain amount of time coaching her, setting her exercises to work out, dictating notes; but in between, he admired her beauty and made her laugh and told her jokes and stories. Once, he even sang her a song. Though every fibre of his body urged him not to hesitate, to grab hold of her and thrust himself on her, he cannily bade his time. Of course, he caressed her, but cautiously, sometimes as if by accident, sometimes playfully, like an uncle.

Theresa enjoyed the company of her uncle immensely. He was the most entertaining tutor she had ever had, a real darling. But he had a strange way of staring at her with unblinking eyes that frightened her sometimes. Her mind was bothered by the prospect of her prelim exam, which was only three weeks away and she knew how little she was prepared for it. She wished at times that he would get on with teaching her and give her more notes so at least she could cram them.

One afternoon, two days after Christmas, Theresa knocked on Erasmo's door and entered his room. He was reclining in bed against a pillow. He had covered himself with a sheet and his chest was bare. He said to her in a soft, sad voice, 'Ah, Theresa, I am so happy to see you today, my dear. Come here and sit beside me. Today we shall have to do our lessons in bed. As you see, I am very ill.'

Theresa offered to leave and let him rest but he said he found it more restful to have her beside him. 'Take off your shoes,' he instructed her and invited her on the bed with all her books. Theresa noticed that his mouth smelt something awful and his eyes were red. But his speech was unslurred, and he spoke carefully, every word like a sigh of relief, or a gentle caress.

'My dear Theresa, what I am about to tell you will be more valuable to you in life than anything you can learn from these books. I know you are worried about your exams. Don't worry. Trust me. Your father has sent you to me because he has trust in me. If you do as I say, you will definitely pass your exam. Today I am going to ask you to do me a good deed, a very big favour. And one good deed, as you know, is worth more in heaven or on earth than all the learning in the world. But first, I will tell you a little about myself. Listen.'

And Erasmo began telling her about his childhood in Goa. He told her about the family house, about the fields around and the servants and the toddy-tappers and the deep blue evening skies that unfolded like a painting, endlessly into eternity. He told her about his mother who died before he could know her, and about his mad father who had hanged himself. And he told her about his cruel sister who was worse than a stepmother, who had raised him and inherited her father's madness. Theresa could not make head nor tail of all this and did not quite believe it all. She wondered what good deed she could possibly do for him, and waited eagerly to oblige. Erasmo was electrified by his own narration.

'I was young and innocent then. There were many things I did not know. And I depended on her to tell me. Who else did I have? For instance, Theresa, I did not know what this was!' Erasmo's voice had grown triumphant and he guided her attention with his eyes to a pointed elevation that had appeared out of nowhere in the sheet that covered his body. His hands were outside. With one hand, he clutched the staff. Theresa stared at it, mystified.

'No, I did not know what this was. Do *you* know what it is?'

Theresa shook her head dumbly.

'So, I showed it to my sister. I asked her to tell me what it was. I danced before her without any clothes on and joyfully revealed it to her. But instead of telling me what it was, she hit me upon it hard, with a pencil that was in her hand and wounded it. I screamed in pain.

'Ever since, my dear, I have been very ill. Very ill. And I shall die soon unless the wound heals... Do you know, Theresa, she keeps me locked up here in this flat. She will not let me go out and meet anyone. Anyway I am too ill now to go anywhere. Only you can cure me, my child, only you can heal this terrible wound.'

'Me?' Theresa asked timidly, pointing to herself.

Erasmo nodded sombrely. The girl asked: 'How?'

Erasmo did not answer. Then he took her hand and held it over the pointed object and said, 'Touch it.'

Theresa was terribly confused and afraid she would burst into tears any minute. She was too timid to oppose Erasmo and he was her uncle after all and perhaps she could help him by doing whatever he asked. But she only half-believed his story. She looked away and touched her hand lightly on the clothed object. It moved.

'Hold it tight,' Erasmo commanded her, and she obeyed.

'To cure it, you must kiss it. Only then will it be healed and I will be well again. I will teach you all that you need to know. And you will most certainly pass your exam.'

Tears rolled down Theresa's cheeks and Erasmo was moved. He kissed her hands and stroked her cheeks and put his lips to her forehead, whispering, 'Help me, Theresa, help me...'

The girl bent down and lightly touched her lips to the thing.

'O my darling, what a great relief. I am feeling so much better. You are so good to me. But dear, to cure it completely you must hold it in your mouth for a few minutes, without any cloth separating your lips from it. It is such an old wound and it will take time to heal.'

Then Erasmo slipped off the sheet and revealed himself to be entirely naked, his penis erect and in full bloom, yearning upward to Theresa's gaping mouth. He put his hands on her head and began to apply a gentle pressure on her to bend. Now the girl was sobbing and twisting her head this way and that, resisting his pressure. In one corner of his fevered consciousness, Erasmo heard the click of a latch turning and remembered with horror that he had not locked the door after Theresa came in. Alberta burst into the room and screamed.

Terror was writ large on her face. As the scene sank in, she gasped, 'Then it's true... it's true...'

Her momentary paralysis lifted and she ordered the girl to get out and go home. Then she removed one shoe from her foot and, getting a good grip on it, she charged at Erasmo and began hitting out wildly at him. On his head, his back, his arms, his face, she hammered away with the stubbed heel of her shoe, all the time shrieking hysterically, 'You evil creature! You mean thing! Get out! Be gone, in the name of the Father, the Son, and the Holy Ghost! Be gone! Leave my brother alone! Leave my brother alone!'

Erasmo cowered with fear, not fighting back, only protecting his organ, which was now limp, with both hands. Then Alberta flung her shoe at Erasmo and burst into pathetic howls, tears of shock and misery streaming down her corpulent cheeks. She ran out of the room, hurriedly crossing herself, slammed

the door shut and threw the bolt from outside. Yevjaan was
kneeling at the altar in the next room, trembling, praying in a
loud quavering voice. Alberta rushed to her and both women
embraced and burst out crying.

It took Alberta three days to find a priest who was willing to
perform an exorcism.

During the last days of December, cold winds blew over
the city. In his room where he had been locked in, Erasmo
seethed and fumed. He paced about day and night naked as
a newborn babe, cursing, swearing, hammering at the door,
threatening to kill himself. He felt neither the cold nor heeded
the aches and groans of his shoe-battered body. His brain was
sharp and alert. Once a day, when they were sure he was not
standing by the door, Alberta would open it a few inches and
slip in a plate of food, with Yevjaan standing by in readiness to
slam it shut again. Erasmo would pick up the plate and fling
it at the door mouthing a string of the vilest abuse, so that
at the end of three days his floor was sprinkled with broken
china splinters which bloodied his feet, and he had not eaten
at all. Now it was all clear to him, clear as daylight. She had
imprisoned him. It was true. And just as he was about to be
healed, she had come charging in to inflict a fresh wound. This
time she would have killed him, too, if he had not protected
himself. Many hours a day, he soothed and stroked his
organ and spoke words of comfort to it and nursed it back to
health. All was not lost yet. He would find a way to escape.
He would be free again, and then nothing could stop him.
Nothing.

On the morning of the last day of the year, Alberta travelled to a distant parish outside Bombay where she met a priest who heard the details of Erasmo's case and agreed that the symptoms were unmistakable, some nasty legionary of the Devil's host had taken possession of her brother's body. He agreed to come to their home that very night to save her brother from its clutches. He said it was a good time to perform an exorcism because the spirit of Christ was still in the air and there was peace and goodwill among men. The forces of evil were at ebb.

That evening Alberta went back to the parish church, which was an hour's ride away by train, to meet the priest and bring him back with her. The priest was an old man, very feeble-looking, and Alberta who had heard tales of the extraordinary strength of possessed people wondered if she had found the right man. But she had no choice now. All she could do was keep faith and pray. The old man kept her waiting a long time as he went doddering about the church packing a bag which contained his articles of holy combat. At last they set out for Byculla. By the time they reached, the festivities had begun in the streets. It was still a few minutes to midnight. People wearing silly plumed hats were playing the fool on the roads, getting ready to blow their paper horns. The lighted Stars of Bethlehem hung from every window. There was a bitter nip in the air.

After crossing himself several times and forbidding the women to enter the room or even to stand near it under any circumstances, the priest flung open Erasmo's door. Inside, Erasmo was lying on his bed naked, masturbating.

The priest, who had a surprisingly deep voice, cried out: 'In the name of Jesus Christ. I command thee evil spirit: Be silent!

Begone! Leave the body of our brother, Erasmo. I command thee in the name of Christ!'

Erasmo let out a terrific roar and jumped out of bed at the priest. The old man yelped in fright and furiously sprinkled holy water on Erasmo, but he had forgotten to latch the door behind him. Erasmo flung the priest aside and ran out, hollering something frightful. He opened the front door and before anyone could stop him, bolted down the stairs, taking three flights at a time. The priest tried to give chase, flinging large quantities of holy water in his direction, waving his crucifix in the air like a wand. But Erasmo was too fast. Within minutes, he had disappeared from sight, down the stairs and out of the building, a strange figure, long-limbed, thin as a skeleton and naked, his big penis bobbing up and down in the air as he ran.

In the street, the midnight hour was approaching. The young children of the neighbourhood had stitched an effigy out of old pillowcases stuffed with rags. They had painted a face on him and dressed him up with a hat and a placard which read, 'Mister Old Man 1983' and tied him to a lamppost. They were waiting impatiently to set the old man on fire. But just as the midnight hour began to strike, the children saw the extraordinary figure of the naked Erasmo racing down the street. Their eyes lit up, they could not believe their luck. A great yelp of joy went up in the air and the children lit their torches and chased the old man into the cold morning of the new year.

The Middle-East Position

KRISHNA SHASTRI DEVULAPALLI

I HAVE A friend. His name is Paddy Padmanabhan. I think everyone should have a friend like Paddy Padmanabhan. Because, in the three decades I've known him, any time life has looked like a subscription unworthy of renewal, Paddy has never failed to give me a story that has made the birds sing again. And these deeply personal life experiences he's shared so selflessly with me usually feature carnivorous wildlife, copious alcohol, sexual depravity of the type that would make Bangkok shudder, Vedic chanting, the local constabulary and his widowed mother, Lalli Mami, in a variety of permutations and combinations all set in exotic locations.

Which is why I sometimes think I should give up everything else and get into the business of being a full-time annalist of Paddy's extraordinary life.

Genre-wise, this true story I'm about to share with you is a multicultural, industrial espionage thriller involving musical interludes, with strong homoerotic overtones and a happy ending.

But not for Paddy.

The cynics among the erotica buffs (and there lurk many, I know) may be of the impression that this is just another loosely strung hack job by an out-of-work author hoping to make a quick couple of thousand quid by duping the editor of an anthology of dubious virtue.

You couldn't be further from the truth.

Putting this piece together has been nothing short of a Bhagiratha-esque penance for its writer. What you are about to read is the outcome of two tortured souls – one, a narrator alternately overcome by grief and relief every thirty seconds or so and, two, a sadomasochistic scribe from the Telugu hinterland dedicated to unearthing the truth at any cost – voluntarily spending three consecutive, harrowing nights in a five-star bar, aided by nothing but single malt and chicken snacks.

Let's begin at the beginning.

Not too long ago, jet-setting executive Paddy Padmanabhan, engineer-founder-CEO of Aanmoolam Technologies (specialists in industrial hygiene & maintenance), was in the Middle East on a business trip. It was night. Meetings had been done, order confirmed and dinner had. In the manner of his Mylaporean brethren, Paddy was Vedically and Vedantically opposed to sleeping with the smell of stale, contraband onion in his room. So he decided to leave the tray of leftover butter nan and chicken do pyaza in the corridor to be cleared by the standard underling sourced from the Malabar coast. But when he stepped out, gently placed the tray down outside his door and turned to go back in, he found he couldn't. Because the door had clicked itself shut.

At this point, Paddy Padmanabhan realised the following:

He'd left his mobile phone in the room.

There was no floor phone in sight.

He was on the sixteenth floor.

He was dressed in shorts and nothing else.

The shorts he was wearing, packed hurriedly by his wife, belonged to his teenage son and were a couple of sizes too small. Owing to his son's love for Tamil kitsch, they had the words 'Big Boy, Mind It!' on them. Also, not that anyone cared, they had a hole in the rear.

Further, his middle-aged torso – as good an example of the Dad Bod as any – was bare except for his snow-white sacred thread.

Finally, thanks to the two beers he'd imbibed without outbibing, he suddenly needed to pee.

In an effort to contain his pulsating bladder, Paddy stood around in the corridor for a few minutes, hopping from foot to foot, reciting in alphabetical order the large repository of devotional hymns at his disposal. When he saw a couple of women getting out of the lift and walking towards him, between chanting achyutam and keshavam, three courses of action presented themselves to him:

1. Pretend he was trying to open the door, in which case the women would see the tear the size of a Murugan idli in the rear of his shorts (his son was also not too hung up on modesty).
2. Casually lean against the door, whistle *The Good, the Bad and the Ugly* (the only international tune he knew), and wait for the women to pass or,
3. Approach the women calmly, tell them of his predicament and seek their assistance.

As the women came closer, Paddy Padmanabhan decided Option 3 was probably the most sensible.

But Paddy did not realise that while considering options 1

and 2, he had actually used them up. This may or may not have had anything to do with the oxygen to his brain being cut off by his stifling of his engorged bladder.

So, instead of seeing a relatively harmless subcontinental on the verge of incontinence, this is what the two Taiwanese/ Chinese women walking up the corridor thought they beheld: a semi-naked man of doubtful naturalisation, his gāngmén partially exposed through a hole in his shorts, rubbing himself against a door, suddenly turning and making a sound like a parakeet being strangled and, before they knew it, God forbid, walking briskly towards them.

So when one of the women yelled 'Lāo piáo!' (which, loosely translated, meant 'brothel frequenter') and unleashed a kick roughly in the direction of the words 'Big Boy' on Paddy's shorts, she couldn't really be blamed.

But, thanks to his luck, the woman's foot missed its target. Which was just as well for all concerned, considering the amount of suppressed liquid nitrogen inside Paddy. But, in the process, her foot got entangled with his sacred thread, making them both fall to the carpeted corridor and Paddy yell 'Shaniyan pudichavalae!' (which, loosely translated, means one possessed by Saturn), instantly undoing whatever sanctity he had garnered via the chanting.

After rolling around in the corridor for a minute or two, her big toe encircled in a death grip by Padmanabhan's sacred thread, the far-eastern woman was disentangled by her companion. In spite of her rigorous training in Tae-Kwon-Do from the age of three, where breaking bricks, deflecting sticks, putting one's limbs through fire and ice, and pushing the mind and body to inhuman limits was a way of life, nothing had prepared the woman for this encounter – having her face sat on by an orthodox South Indian Brahmin male rear for an entire minute.

So, when her friend separated her from Paddy, instead of taking a deep breath and finishing off her untrained, physically inferior opponent who was on all-fours with two swift moves, the woman hobbled away, defeated, sobbing and babbling unintelligibly. But all the fighting, rolling, kicking, biting, sobbing and cursing in two distinctly different languages yielded a result. A door opened.

Paddy looked up to see a man in a thobe, the traditional Arab gear, but more importantly, a bathroom clearly visible in the background. The non-musical version of Vegas's famous Bellagio fountain inside him threatened to come on.

'May I use your bathroom, please?' Paddy said. Introductions, nature of business, and enquiries of net worth could wait.

To Paddy's delight, the man said 'Be my guest' in English with a pleasing Middle-Eastern accent. His expression gave no indication of surprise or enquiry with regard to Paddy's minimalist get-up.

Paddy Padmanabhan rushed into the loo and unclenched his tortured sphincter. In the soul-satisfying 120 seconds it took him to empty the contents of his bladder, and rather carelessly at that, with an estimated spatter-dia of eighteen inches, Paddy noticed the following – there were bruises on his upper body caused by the nails, feet and fists of the Taiwanese/Chinese woman, the bathroom of his saviour had a feminine, lavendery fragrance, and what sounded like Cerrone's *Love in C Minor* wafted in from the room on the other side of the door.

'All okay?' said the Arab from outside.

'Thanks. Just some minor bruises,' said Paddy, sighing, watching his dying golden shower with something like affection. 'I'll attend to them as soon as I get a duplicate key from the reception.'

'No need for that. We can attend to them right here. I have just the balm,' said the man.

'Thanks,' said Paddy.

Who said Arabs were rude and unhelpful?

Paddy stepped out, let out another sigh, and looked at his new host's room for the first time. He had to admit it was beautifully appointed. There was a tasteful flower arrangement. The giant bed had red satin sheets. On a table by its side, there was a bottle of champagne in an ice bucket and two flutes. But for some reason, the door that had saved him a moment ago was shut and a table had been dragged across to block it. And his kindly Arab samaritan was reclining on a love seat, an economy-sized tube of gel in one hand and his uneconomical and somewhat misshapen erection in the other.

'Big boy, eh?' said the Arab, pointing to the legend on what remained of Paddy's shorts. Then he squeezed a huge blob of bluish petroleum jelly on to his hand and said, 'Enough?'

'No, sir, I mean, yes, sir... don't, sir,' said Paddy in a voice octave-wise somewhere between Manmohan Singh and Sachin Tendulkar. While he had never employed the product in his own sporadic, predictable and foreshortened sex life, he *was* aware of its uses. Thanks to the browser history on his son's computer, he had, through a series of riveting six-seven minute clips involving the athletic, and sometimes inexplicable, efforts of M/s Leone, Rai, Olsen & Co, been left in no doubt whatsoever about the versatility of the glutinous medium.

'C'mon,' said the man, pointing yet again to Paddy's shorts. 'We all know big boys like it.'

'Oh, that-aa? Summa, thamash,' (loosely translated: Nothing. Just) said Paddy, trying to distance himself from the tagline on his shorts. What was wrong with his son? If he made it back home, he would cut him off from his will *and cut off his priapic pee-pee*, the kazhudey!

Why had things come to such a pass? Had he not been a model member of his community that morning? Hadn't he said his prayers, touched his widowed mother's feet, and used only one cuss word at his wife when a beating was what she was asking for? And hadn't he managed to avoid both rahu kalam and yama gandam successfully while catching his flight? And yet, here he was, a heartbeat away from having a spontaneous Middle-Eastern style colorectal to the beat of Cerrone. Dammit, it had to be the vastu of his hotel room. The bloody toilet was in the north-east. He'd have to kill his travel agent if he ever got out of this with his honour intact.

As his would-be molester threw his thobe away with surprising daintiness and proceeded to rotate his member like the blade of a windmill at what looked like sixty-five rpm with minimal hip movement (a move known in erotic/pornographic circles simply as the 'helicopter'), Paddy decided to give saving his virtue one last try.

'Sir,' he said, 'are you religious?'

The Middle-Eastern man stopped the penile swivelling, brought his blurry member to a gradual standstill and looked up at the ceiling, hands outstretched.

'Yes, very much,' he said. 'I am a god-fearing man.'

'In that case… er…' said Paddy. The idea forming in his head was definitely unconventional. But that was all he had. '…you see, sir,' he said, 'according to our scriptures, no South

Indian man of the priestly class is allowed to even fantasise about having sex with another man unless...'

'Unless?' said the host.

Paddy wondered why he'd said 'unless'. 'Unless... unless... the other man is at least a first-class cricketer with a high back-lift and a copybook cover drive.'

The would-be molester scratched his off-kilter testicles thoughtfully and considered Padmanabhan's words for a moment.

'My friend, I see your problem,' he said. 'The good book, no matter which faith it belongs to, must be respected. Worry no more. I won't make violent and repeated love to you all night.'

'Thank you, sir,' said Paddy, involuntarily reaching for his visiting card and realising he was semi-naked. He felt the need to make a token gesture of gratitude to the man who had put off his molestation for the moment.

'Please visit us,' he said, 'when you come to Madras. We will show you the Marina and Vandalur Zoo...'

'Instead... instead...,' said the man.

Paddy's brief moment of rectal relief disappeared. What *was* the instead? Was it something worse, something beyond the realm of his son's browsing history? Was it something even Ms Khalifa wouldn't attempt? Maybe he'd been hasty in inviting the Arab home. Say, the Arab perpetrated the 'instead' *and* took him up on his invite? It would be embarrassing introducing him to his mother. What would he say? Amma, please meet my new friend, Mr So-and-So. Just a couple of days ago, he cured me of my chronic constipation?

'Instead,' said the man, 'there's no reason why we can't have a couple of slow dances, right? At least, for starters. Have some champagne... let the night take its course?'

To Paddy's despair, offhand he couldn't find anything in the scriptures that forbade the priestly class from slow-dancing with a naked Arab.

'I suppose so,' he said, '... but... you *have* to change the music.'

'Sure,' said the Arab, fingering his playlist. 'Bollywood? Hip-Hop? *Barry White*?'

'Got any Air Supply?' said Paddy. He had always liked *Lost in Love*. *I Love the Rainy Nights* was good, too. Or was that Eddie Rabbit?

'Have *I* got Air Supply?' said the Arab. 'You kidding? I saw them perform, my friend! I have their *Live in Wembley*.'

'Cool,' said Paddy. Maybe he could ask him to copy the album on his pen drive.

'Hey,' said the Arab as *All out of Love* came on. 'I get to lead, okay?'

Who was he, a mere industrial hygienist from Madras, a second-class pass from REC, Trichy, to argue with an ambanam Arab wielding a semi-erect penis?

'Sure, why not?' said Paddy.

So, unknown to his widowed mother, wife and friends from the Rotary Club in Madras, on the sixteenth floor of a reputed hotel in the Gulf, the five feet five inches tall CEO of Aanmoolam Tech, dressed in tiny, torn shorts, and a Middle-Eastern man in a shaggy birthday suit held each other for their first slow dance of the evening.

'But first, a selfie, okay, for FB?' said the Arab putting his grizzled cheek to his companion's baby soft one and turning his camera phone towards them.

'Smile,' he said.

Paddy gave his best smile, and the Arab sucked in his cheeks and pouted when there was a 'phut' followed by another 'phut'. As the Arab suddenly became heavier in his arms, Paddy realised there was a bindi in the middle of his companion's forehead and a red trickle was oozing out of it.

It took Paddy three seconds to realise that someone had cut in on their dance. With a bullet.

It was at this point Paddy realised forces larger than improper vastu were at play. Had he only taken cognizance of maternal aunt Pattu's prediction of a fortnight ago and gone to the Adi Kumbeshwarar temple and donated a cow and a year's worth of fodder to a poor brahmin, would a woman who was a dead-ringer for his watchman Bahadur have attacked him without preamble, or a priapic Arab tried to take his virtue, or would he, for that matter, be in the pose he was in now: like Clark Gable in the poster of *Gone With The Wind* holding a recumbent Vivien Leigh who in his case was a hairy dead man with an erection?

It was his jatakam.

He wasn't responsible for the smiley-faced corpse in his arms or any of the other stuff. He was just an innocent bystander caught in the crossfire of the interplanetary gang war in his horoscope.

A guttural voice said, 'Iskat yego!'

Paddy dropped his defunct dance partner to the floor and turned around. He didn't know the words meant 'Search him!' in Russian but he did know, better than ever, that Pattu Chitthi had got it bang on.

Two men, one, roughly the size, and colour, of his Samsung 440-litre energy-saving fridge, and another, slightly smaller, but equally frosty, stood by an open door on the other side of the room. The smaller of the two held a weapon with a silencer that was still smoking.

There was another door? How come he hadn't noticed it?

Without too much ceremony, the big one turned the Arab around, put on a rubber glove that he'd whipped out, and put his hand deep into whatever there was between the Arab's rear cheeks. As he moved his hand this way and that with the delicacy of an archaeologist at a new dig, he gave Paddy a wink. Paddy heard a swoosh. It was the sound of his own testicles disappearing into their childhood hiding place. After a few seconds, the man's gloved hand emerged. Paddy opened one eye to see what it had found.

It looked like a condom filled with something and tied up at one end.

'That's half. Where's the rest?' said the little guy.

The two men looked at each other and looked at Paddy.

'Turn around and bend,' said the big guy.

Paddy wondered at how strange life was. That morning, as he was driving past Valluvar Kottam, would he have known that there was a thriving subculture in the Middle East which had an acute interest in his anus? The Chinese woman, the Arab and now a Russian – all interested in getting to his tonsils via the scenic route.

How bad could it be? He remembered how, in class six, when he'd stood up yet again to be the first to answer a question in Maths class, his classmate Dhandapani had put an upright, sharpened Nataraj pencil in the path to his seat. He had had to take two weeks off.

Paddy took a deep breath, cursed his wife silently and turned around.

'Someone's already got to it, boss,' the big guy said.

'How?' asked big guy.

Through the corner of his eye, Paddy figured they were referring to the gaping hole in his shorts.

There is a limit for every man. This was mine. Pushing my single malt aside, I cut in.

'Enough, da,' I said. 'Let's leave the story here. I'll fill in the gaps.'

Fill in the gaps? Is that what I'd actually said? How insensitive could I be?

'No, wait,' said Paddy. 'This is the best part...'

I looked into Paddy's eyes, glazed *and* bloodshot by three days of drinking, weeping and recollecting. My super-homophobic friend *had* changed. Hitherto, the best parts of all his previous stories involved money, female cleavage, or money being stuffed into female cleavage. And here he was, on the verge of recounting a rectal Russian roulette encounter, with himself at the business end.

I braced myself for a hard landing.

'So the Russian looks at my hole, the one in the shorts that is, and picks up the gel...' said Paddy.

'Let's stop here,' I said. What holy river could I go to to wash myself of this? There was only so much I could compromise for free booze. How would I ever be able to look at Lalli Mami again?

'Then, just like that, out of the blue, the other guy, remember there were two Russians...'

Oh, god, this was getting worse. Who would've thought that, out there in the world of oil and sand, there were not one, not two, but three men who man-lusted after my poor classmate?

Paddy continued.

'The other guy looks at me and says, "Are you from Chennai?"'

'The Russian?' I asked.

'Obviously,' he said. 'Not the dead Arab.'

'Then?'

'Then what? I said I was. He said don't you remember me? I said no. He said he was formerly with Zhivago Technologies, the purchase manager. Didn't I remember meeting him in Minsk? I said, of course, I did and it all came back to me. Three years ago we'd done some work for a petrochemical guy there...'

'Wait,' I said. 'You're telling me the Russian hit-man who'd just anally violated a dead Arab was your *client*?'

'Yes,' he said. 'Why not? Lots of people do two jobs. My uncle Varadarajan, for instance, is a chartered accountant by day and a go-go dancer by night.'

'So your story ends there, thank god. The guy let you off,' I said. I could face Lalli Mami, after all. Her son was still pure.

'Not exactly,' said Paddy Padmanabhan.

'There's more?'

'Yes,' said Paddy. 'The Russian. Boris Jakov, yes, that's his real name. Well, he and his wife want to tour the temples in the Kumbakonam area because she apparently has a dosham in her horoscope that makes her barren. I have been asked to arrange the whole thing...'

'Oh? His wife is Indian?'

'No,' said Paddy. 'Taiwanese. Turns out she's the woman I'd sat on earlier. Well, let's pray she keeps it our little secret.'

Insomnia

MITALI SARAN

AT FIRST MILI sleeps deeply and awakes refreshed, with only a vague sense that her memory of the night is incomplete. When she washes the night out of her eyes, it is with an expression that will become a frown when her face ages a little, as if she's trying to work out what she's missed. But a shake of the head and the morning breeze is enough to dispel the feeling.

Gradually, over a few weeks, she becomes aware that she is dreaming turbulently each night, but her recollections are riddled with doubt. Disturbing, shadowy images appear now and again, triggered by inconsequential thoughts and events, but she can make no complete picture of them.

Then, one day, she's having lunch with her husband Rudra and her old friend Nish, in a small restaurant they've frequented for years. The familiar beige and white checked linen and fresh red roses, the large smudged window, the smell of coffee and a menu that hasn't changed in a decade, make them more languorous than the wine and sunlight.

Nish's hand moves through the air as she talks, wrist thin and translucent, blue cigarette smoke pirouetting in a bar of light.

– A few secrets, and a little space, she concludes. Isn't that what we all want?

Her arm describes a circle, the white blouse lifting against the light to outline the shape of her body beneath. As her arm comes down, two fingers accidentally graze Rudra's skin, on the biceps below the T-shirt sleeve. It is less than a second before Nish's hand is back on the table before the vee of her neckline, where the skin is no longer tan.

In that second, Mili's mind dissolves. She feels the blood rush to her face in the same instant its pounding drowns out the sound of Nish's voice. Enveloped in silence, in slow motion, Mili watches carefully: she sees the smoke snaking up, the shining dark red of Nish's mouth thrown open in laughter, the skin on her husband's arm breaking into goose pimples under the long white fingers. She notices Rudra's wet lips and the vein on his temple. She faces them, Nish talking, slowing, stopping.

– Good heavens, Mil, are you alright? You look as if you've seen a ghost!

– Darling, are you ill?

Mili stares at them and sees Nish's tongue sliding over her husband's belly and down his flanks. She sees his hands clutching and pulling at her breasts, eyes glazed. She sees Nish panting above him, gripping his hair. She hears him growl. She realises she has dreamt this.

In the same moment that pain goes tearing through her heart, stopping her breath, she feels with a shock that her underwear is moistening against her thin cotton skirt and the cheap plastic chair. Mili's eyes are paralysed with pain. She swallows, pushes the chair out behind her, stands abruptly. A fiery line is pulsing from her belly to her groin.

– Excuse me, she says, back in a minute.

She walks fast, shaking with anxiety. In the small bathroom she closes the door gently and leans against it. After a few moments she turns on the tap and splashes her face with water, and then she can't help it. She runs her damp hands over her neck and into her blouse, she's picking up her own skirt; she sits on the counter and swings her legs up and her tongue licks her own tongue in the mirror. Her hands are moving fast. She remembers dreaming of her husband and Nish fucking in her own bedroom, on the sheets Mili bought herself at a sale, and the force of her orgasm makes her bite her lip.

When she returns to the table, cheeks pink, hair patted back into place, clothes rumpled, they both reach for her hands.

– Are you alright? asks Rudra. You look a little dizzy.

– I slipped in the loo, she says, laughing. The floor was wet. Aren't I a mess!

The meal is over; they kiss goodbye. Mili inhales as she leans towards Nish, taking in the powdery smell of her cheek and hair. She kisses her on the neck, where the ear joins the jaw, and has to stop herself from sucking the skin. She withdraws, and watches Nish's mouth part involuntarily as Rudra leans in to say goodbye, lips briefly touching her cheek.

After this Mili can rarely sleep well. When she does, the dreams fill her nights like bright, poisonous flowers, as vivid and beautiful as they are deadly. She dreams of betrayal in the most outlandish detail, in the most impossible circumstances. Her waking hours are spent reliving the night. While her husband is at work she stands at the window, wondering if he's really at work. She cries often.

Sometimes she dreams of watching her husband convulse inside Nish whose fingers are in his mouth. She wakes at night to find that she has come in her sleep, growing aware of the contractions as they die away. She rises to drink some water and finds her bedsheet moist beneath her, next to where Rudra is sleeping with his back to her.

Mili can't bring herself to tell her husband. Her eyes grow dark with shadows. She is sick with pain, but the more it hurts, the more she is aroused. If Rudra discovers that she knows, he might break off his affair. When he reaches for her in bed she is stricken with guilt. He squeezes and kneads her, the way she likes him to, and whispers in her ear: I want you, dirty little slut, the way she likes him to, but she remains tense and dry. He climbs on top of her, whispering, trying to excite her, grinding his hips against hers, biting her throat, growling, the way she likes him to, but he cannot make her wet.

Only with a supreme effort of concentration can she shut out his voice, and rifle through the growing catalogue of her dreams to pick one that will send her over the edge. She might think of the dream in which Rudra is sitting clothed on a chair, with Nish kneeling between his legs. She sees Nish mouthing her husband, saliva silvering her lips, and she wants to touch Nish.

Her desire rises, and beneath her husband's body she starts to respond. He encourages her, and she squeezes her eyes shut to better focus on her dream while he pounds at her body. She is surprised at the speed and violence of her orgasm.

After breakfast one day, Rudra stands over her as Mili makes a phone call to a reputed doctor for an appointment. He looks at her worriedly over his shoulder as he leaves for work.

– Sweetheart, he says, don't forget that medical checkup. Your health is getting out of hand.

She has seen a very faint stain on his neck, well below the shirt collar. Her eyes are cupped in blued skin from lack of sleep and her hair is lank from neglect.

An hour later the phone rings. It is Nish. They have not met since that lunch all those weeks ago, but Nish has invaded the house permanently. Hearing her voice, Mili panics.

– Where have you been?

– Life is so busy, says Mili, her heart hammering. And Rudra is working so much.

– So what, says Nish, let's you and I have some lunch.

They arrange to meet at the same place. Mili is in a flutter of indecision. After trying on four or five outfits she dresses carefully, choosing a thin-strapped black halter that shows off her shoulders and pale long neck, with a mid-length black skirt and heels. She has washed her hair for the first time in days, fussing over a selection of clips and hairbands before deciding to pin it up simply. She chooses a pale pink lipstick with lots of shine and makes her eyes up to hide the shadows. She takes a little black wrap against the cool winter air. Motorists on the road look into her car and watch her eyes dart up to the rear-view mirror as she checks her hair nervously.

Nish is already seated at their favourite table in a plunging, cross-strapped white dress that is slit in the back to mid-thigh. She is a tall woman, about the same height and as dark-haired and pale-skinned as Mili. Her lashes, thick with mascara, shadow the upper half of her pupils. Her lipstick is deep red, as always.

She rises to greet Mili with frank surprise in her eyes.

– You look fabulous! I spoke to Rudra the other day, I think you were in bed, and he said he was a little worried about you, but you look fine. Since when did you become so sexy?

Mili smiles and drops her gaze in confusion. She knows that Nish is lying; in the last few weeks, she has never gone to bed before her husband, and she could never have slept through a phone call. It doesn't matter; all she wants is to play along, to be beautiful and agreeable and included.

They order a bottle of white wine and drain the first glass, giggling like schoolgirls. Mili finds herself flirting, glancing sideways at Nish, touching her own neck and throat, adjusting her top so that it falls lower on her chest, tinkling at her jokes, talking too much about nothing. Their booth is at the back of the restaurant, behind a set of pillars. Mili feels as if they are alone; she is blooming. Nish is looking at her with a strange expression, half-amazed.

— I'm glad Rudra isn't here, she says suddenly. We haven't met like this, just the two of us, in years!

— Yes, says Mili. God knows we love him, but why can't a man be more like a woman?

She looks up into Nish's eyes, and realises that her hunger shows. The wine has warmed her veins. Mili takes her life in her hands and reaches across the table to touch Nish's fingers. She plays with them a little, hesitantly, stroking the skin and the edges of the nails, just as if she were admiring the varnish. She squeezes her chest between her arms to deepen her cleavage. She doesn't dare look up.

— Excuse me? The waiter startles them. Would you like to order?

His eyes are riveted upon their gently laced fingertips. They place their orders and wait for him to leave. Once he's gone and they are alone, Mili is buffeted by such shame and guilt that her ears ring. She murmurs,

— Listen, I'm sorry, I just...

— No, Nish replies, don't say that.

Mili looks up. She raises Nish's hand to her lips and takes

a fingertip tentatively in her mouth. Her friend's breathing goes ragged. Nish withdraws her finger and puts it into her own mouth. They look at each other, lips wet, and rise together. They half-walk, half-stumble into the ladies' room and lock the door.

Their breathing is filled with gasps as they kiss, hair coming undone, throats reddened under bites, straps hanging off their shoulders. Mili, thinks of Rudra, and wants to make Nish cry with pleasure. She feels ashamed, and filthy, and madly, madly aroused. They collapse on the floor, Mili whispering,

– I want to hear you come.

Skin pearled with perspiration, mouth on lips and breasts, fingers under the white dress. She listens to Nish's sounds and smells her and plays with her, pushing and pulling back, nipping at her throat. Very quickly Nish's eyes squeeze shut and she gasps and comes noisily, lying in a rigid arc on the bathroom floor. Mili begins to move against her. She thinks of Rudra and feels terrible shame. It makes her wild. I want to fuck you like a man, she whispers, the way Rudra fucks you. The shock on Nish's face, so weak beside her desire, sends Mili over the edge and she closes her eyes.

After a few minutes they stand shakily, pat down hair and dresses. They can't look at each other; they will eat just a few mouthfuls of food in silence, until Nish drops her cutlery abruptly, rises from her chair, and excuses herself.

Mili will finish her meal, looking out the window with eyes like open wounds. She knows she will not see Nish again for a long time. She will go to the doctor if Rudra insists. She thinks she will sleep quietly again.

The Last House

RUPA BAJWA

JHARNA LET OUT a closed-up sigh when she shut the door behind her. With the door, she also shut out her noisy, sweaty, crowded and demanding world behind her. Her taut body recognised the silence and her tightened, knotted up spine relaxed with half-pleasure and half-pain.

The apartment felt cool and peaceful, as it always did. Jharna had taken a bath that morning, scrubbing herself hard with the dried, fissured, orange bar of soap, trying to scrub her cracked, grimy heels and wash herself as best she could in the cramped cement enclosure with the ice-cold water. But now it had been several hours since her bath.

After feeding her children, packing lunch for her husband for his factory lunch break, travelling in a crowded bus from her slum to Kaveri Apartments in Vasant Kunj, she had worked in three houses. The bath seemed ages ago. The smells of frying oil, onions she had chopped, disinfectant that the madam in flat 363 insisted on using, and the smells of her own body – sweat, stale talcum powder and her amla hair oil – had become trapped in her green nylon sari. She always became aware of her odour in this apartment because there was nothing here to disguise it – no perfumes, no air freshener, no feminine odour, no smells at all.

She felt grimy and smelly and her feet ached.

But this was the last house.

And he lived here.

❧

He had moved in a month ago. She had seen the transport truck moving and stopping in front of that gate from Mrs Kapoor's kitchen window, where she was drying her irritatingly heavy china plates. As soon as she got off work, she hurried to his house. She had already noticed the absence of any marks of a woman or a child's presence in the household. She knew he'd need a maid and had hurried to get the job before it could be snapped up by anyone else. A single man would be easy to work for. How much cooking and cleaning could he need? He offered her a wooden stool to sit on, remaining standing himself. The apartment was sparely furnished. Jharna assumed it was because the moving men were still walking in and out, their boots making a clattering sound on the bare floor. But she was later to know that he had very few possessions. He was quiet and spoke to her respectfully. She had looked up at his lean face as he spoke to her, explaining his few simple needs. Then he asked her a question and she realised she had not been listening. She shook herself, trying to get herself into her usual, sharp, survival-professional mode. Even that did not seem very necessary with him, for they settled on a fairly generous salary and she could dispense with the haggling for-a-higher-salary-with-new-employer ritual. She realised he was expecting her to leave, after they had decided on a time that suited them both, and as she got to her feet, his stubble, his voice, his very presence gave her goosebumps and trembling knees. She had fairly fled.

That had been four months ago. For the first few days, Jharna had felt very guilty. She had a fairly decent husband. He never hit her, did not drink, did not ask her for money or bully her. She had known no anguish with him but had known no raptures or ecstasies either. He was used to routine daily sex with her, after which he would have a couple of beedis and then go to sleep. She knew nothing of the tortures some of her female friends described, who went through agonising, demanding acts by their husbands. She had become used to being more or less grateful for the gentle husband and her three children, a result of their uneventful unions.

And now, her toad-like docility had been disturbed by this man, who had never even so much as made the slightest pass at her. She, who had been trained by her mother, and then later by her mother-in-law, to keep an eye out for the slightest sign of lechery by her male employers, had slipped into an easy, happy carelessness while working at his place, cheerfully cleaning, cooking and scrubbing while he typed at his computer, sometimes muttering to himself, and only emerging occasionally to ask for a cup of tea or coffee, arousing more a maternal instinct in her than anything else. And yet, yes, sometimes more than a maternal instinct, for when her defences were down, she'd notice his throat, his lock of hair that fell over his forehead, his deep voice…

And then, slowly, over the ensuing months, Jharna realised that the maternal instinct was not the whole truth. She had trained herself so well to anticipate and resist male advances that she barely knew what to feel when the training was not needed.

When she encountered such a strange, alien creature like this man… Jharna felt guilty and uncertain for some weeks. Then, as her body, skin, hair and breath seemed to come alive one by one, she gave up the guilt and waited each day for the hour and a half when she could be close to him. After cooking and cleaning for him Jharna went home, with a strange feeling of bliss and some confusion, as she tried to understand the weird joy and calmness that could arise from cleaning a man's dishes, home and clothes.

The time at his place became a beautiful, tortured interlude in Jharna's otherwise exhausting, similar days. She had no idea that he had begun to watch and wait too.

One day she reached his place feeling tired of the noise at her home, the lack of comfort (not material comfort, but the comfort she felt her husband should be giving her, in words and touch). He told her he had to leave but instead of cooking, could she please sort out his woollens today (the last left cupboard in his bedroom)? Air them, fold them and put them in again? She nodded listlessly. While he spoke she noticed his wrists, his long fingers, his slightly and strangely calloused hands. She wondered how they would feel to touch. He gathered a sheaf of papers from his desk and left the house, closing the door quietly after him. Jharna looked after him in longing and exasperation. Why, why, oh WHY did he have to be a sahib? Anyway, she got to work till she chanced upon a long, dark, warm coat of his. She could smell his vague scent on it. She caressed it with her fingers. The collar, the sleeves, the beautiful himness of it. It felt huge and warm to touch. She stood there and before she knew it, she had tears streaming down her eyes. She buried her face in the warm, woollen, navy blue depths. She felt the alien, luxurious fabric rough against her face and throat. Her skin prickled. She reluctantly held the coat slightly away from her body. It was beautiful. And large. And all-enveloping. Jharna sank on a chair with the coat in her lap. She sat there for ages and got up in a panic when the doorbell rang. It was another of the strange parcels he received, full of books.

'Sign?' the delivery boy said laconically and with a slight challenge. She said nothing. With the coat draped over her elbow, she felt like another woman. She threw back the challenge with her eyes without saying anything, a challenge born of an inexplicable new-found confidence.

The boy shrugged, took away the unsigned paper and left.

However, the feeling of well-being vanished the next day. She had bought vegetables and straggled into the kitchen, weighed down by them. She divested herself of the plastic bags of groceries, of those spilling over with vegetables. A tomato rolled to her feet. He bent and picked it up, his index finger brushing her silver toe rings as he did so. The touch sent a tremor up her feet to her to body. He noticed and stood up straight, confusedly handing the tomato to her. His own hands were trembling slightly. There was something so foreign about the touch of her skin, of the feel of the cold metal on her toe.

Jharna had, however, felt the high heat of his skin on hers. 'Sahib, you have a fever?' she asked anxiously.

'Yes,' he said, with a sheepish face. 'Just flu or something. I'll be fine.'

But as she worked in the kitchen, he grew worse. When she went to tell him that she was leaving, he was lying in his bedclothes, shivering. Jharna panicked. Immediately.

She ran back to the kitchen and brought a basin of water and a flannel. She began to sponge his forehead. He protested weakly at first, and then gave in. Jharna became immune to time and her surroundings. All she could sense was the heat and the water. She sponged his neck, his beautiful palms, the reassuring soles of his feet. Half an hour passed before she knew it. The water grew warm every five minutes and she went to change it. He could feel his fever going down, very, very slowly. But there was a difference. Jharna came back and wrung the flannel out again, the lines of worry on her face having eased a little now. He looked down at the woman staring intently at his feet, her kohl smudged, her bindi a little askew now, her cheap blue sari with little red flowers on it splattered with water. And he almost knew. Before he could think the thought through, she was kissing the soles of his feet between sponging them. He felt as he had never felt before, never with his 'normal', unmarried, educated girlfriends. He closed his eyes as he felt the caresses of her hands climb up his body. The boundaries between them blurred as they often are by common human illnesses; they were soon in each other's arms. She was still trying to sponge him when the flannel fell away on the bed. He was soon nuzzling the soft insides of her elbows, touching the bare back between her sari and her blouse, till all off-limit places disappeared, the two clinging to each other, their clothes having magically followed the discarded flannel, their skins feeling each other with a quiet urgency, the two unaware of how and when their fevers had become one.

The bedsheets were warm and crumpled. A pigeon sat at the window.

She went home, uncomfortable in the bus, uncomfortable in the narrow lane that led to her small quarters, uncomfortable once amidst her family. She felt certain everyone would be able to smell him on her body.

Feel the heat of his fever in her.

She took a towel and a change of clothes and went for an untimely bath.

The next day, she rang his doorbell with terrible nervousness. He opened the door and behaved as if nothing had happened, though his face was strangely gentle. He seemed still slightly unwell and feverish and was silently typing away at his computer when she brought him his usual cup of tea, only with some tulsi leaves boiled in it to make his throat better. She was anxious. Would he fire her? He clasped the cup handle gingerly and took a sip. She hesitated, then turned and went back to the kitchen, swinging between disappointment and relief. Soon, she heard the tapping noise of his typing resume.

Jharna carefully sliced off the ends of a clove of unpeeled garlic, her hands trembling. Then she chopped it into tiny pieces. After she was done, she took up a gnarly ginger root, as if she were sleepwalking. She held it in the hollow of her palm, its roughness against her skin reminding her of his beautiful stubble. She tried not to think of it and sensibly managed to grate some of the ginger.

Then she managed to snap out of her spell. She rapidly cooked masoor dal, sprinkled dhania over it, boiled rice, and then scrubbed the kitchen counters clear. A lump in her throat, she quickly swept and scrubbed the floors of all three rooms, including his, where he typed without looking at her, and then she stood up.

'I am leaving, Sahib. Anything else?'

'No,' he said, in a low voice. 'Thank you, Jharna. The tea eased my throat.'

Jharna left.

Things went back to the way they were, both of them behaving as if nothing had happened.

One day he told her he had finished writing his book. She looked at his face blankly. A whole book! Then he said he had rented the apartment just to finish it and that he would be leaving.

'I thought I should tell you. So you can look for work in this time slot.'

She nodded.

The day he was to leave, Jharna helped him fold all his clothes while he put them away. Men were carrying boxes of books and the few pieces of furniture to a hired tempo downstairs. He fumbled with his wallet, took out a five-hundred rupee note and handed it to her. She began to protest. But he interrupted her. 'Diwali is coming up,' he said. 'Please buy toys or clothes for your children.'

Then he turned and went out. She followed him. The man that the landlord had sent locked the empty apartment.

Jharna watched silently as he disappeared into the lift with the landlord's man.

Jharna went home. That evening, when she was cooking on the kerosene stove, she remembered his touch on her body. Again. She told her children she would be coming back home earlier for a few days, till she found another house.

Her last house was empty.

Thy Will Be Done

SHINIE ANTONY

WHEN MY SISTERS wearied of finding love, battling as they were long-drawn goodbyes in inappropriate alliances, a visiting aunt had said: 'You find the wrong man but the right man finds you.'

My father, a godman of some repute, had rallied his best against our hormones – after, no doubt, recovering from the shock of producing nothing but daughters four – by instilling in us a disdain of the body, of the merely physical, corporeal, material. We lived a frugal life, with the feasts thrown now and then by the more affluent of his followers the only gastronomic dazzle. Our clothes were hand-me-downs, hair butchered at the neck by Mother on the first Sunday of every month and ornaments, if any, a rudraksh or red thread on the wrist.

Father would line us up once in a while, his frown clearing only when it travelled up, up to our heads. As long as we had no hair we were safe. No man would want us, no man would look at us.

Despite Father's strictest admonishments two of my sisters managed to elope; one with an elderly bigamous gentleman and the other with one of those scruffy elements who seemed open to robbing houses and chain-snatching. Both sisters disappeared overnight. One night there they were, shifty-eyed, whining over the same poha being served, next night poof. Father never fully recovered and spent his last days muttering about conspiracies and plots. He had always had a fertile imagination when it came to enmities, having relentlessly advised people on black magic. His worst nightmare had come true – his daughters had let him down because they were daughters and not sons, girls and not boys. The tumour that took him almost incidental, he died more from a deep abiding disappointment with himself.

My youngest sister's mind had stopped at age four. At thirty she giggled and threw fits when the mood took her. Great care was taken to not set her off. But there were still times when her expressions were completely out of context. At the funeral she laughed uproariously, ate all the food offerings with gusto, licking her fingers one by one ostentatiously, and sang the bhajans in a loud lilting voice, clapping her hands and asking others to join in as Father used to. 'Poor thing,' people said, shaking their heads.

Attempts were made to make me the head of the set-up and though I first couldn't believe this and was repulsed by the idea, I soon saw some merit in it. I already knew the workings and mechanisms of running the place, I knew the stock phrases and prayers, I could face-read and advice up to a point and, as I belatedly remembered, I had to eat. Plus, unlike my father, I could read and Google and reach the English-speaking crowds easily. In a month's time I had two cell phones and a small coterie around me who consulted me on matters cosmic. And I who had never given a thought to the future was surprisingly articulate on the fate of just about everything and everyone.

I was especially popular for my encompassing talks, where I quoted – in the most inoffensive manner possible – from all scriptures, and focused mainly on the feel-good factor for my herd. Little Krishna, Infant Jesus. I preferred gods in their childhoods, at their innocent best, in a crib, on a lap.

I moved downstairs, to where Father used to stay, and my mother and volatile sister stayed upstairs. Since I was now the breadwinner and a semi-important person, there was a necessary reserve between me and the rest of the family. As a soothsayer I needed privacy and respect, and no cottage industry can survive interfering kith and kin. And thus it was that at the age of thirty-four I found myself irrevocably unloved.

Anything faintly illicit was sure to be sniffed out by the tight circles around me and the matter of bread and butter would collapse like someone's last breath. There was that time when a young NRI boy was brought to me by his anxious father. We sat undisturbed in a room with the door shut and I was supposed to bring him back to his senses following a failed affair. But the more I watched his face grow animated as he spoke of his passion, the more I wanted… I don't know what. The whole night I was restless, feverish. The next morning I asked the boy to be called back. This time in the room I touched his hand as if absently, even maternally. And when he did not jerk back or scream for help, I stroked his hand and stopped only when my own hand started to tremble.

I waited for the rogue blood to flow out of my veins. I prayed. I fasted. But all the serenity I could muster felt like someone else's skin. I longed instead for the tossing and turning, for the I don't know what.

❦

'Krishna and Christ, so many similarities! Both born on chaotic nights, hunted as babies, brought up by foster dads. And look at how important wood turned out to be for both of them: a flute for one and a cross for the other. That is how we remember them, with hands on a flute and hands on a cross.'

I speak fluently but like a recording – for all of a sudden I am without an axis. From the moment I woke up there was this dizzy, as if my insides cart-wheeled. Putting on a blouse had taken forever, fingers dawdling longer and longer at each button. When the door opened I'd sat up guiltily.

For days I keep myself together, give nothing away. I dare not close my eyes even to sleep! I listen with excess care to what someone is saying lest I smile when not meant to. It is difficult though to dole out advice, to nod understandingly, to inhabit the boring old world of others. For I've met you at last and having met you there's no way I can un-meet you now.

By the time the car comes to take a chief-guest me to the city college I sense your impatience, a mirror image of mine. As I enter the premises there is a holding of breath and I am careful not to let my fingers brush any part of me lest I catch fire. That is how I know you are here, at my lecture, watching me, studying me, not taking your eyes off me for a second and I almost falter. I cannot look at you, though you wait all the while, willing me to raise my gaze.

The day is long, the queue of devotees waiting for me longer. They are the reason I smile and talk and go about my business. But you? You are why I am.

A curtain rustles, the clock ticks, a candle drips wax, and quiet as a soul exits a body you enter my room. I don't turn around. I only know. The length of your eyelash, the palm out to catch me like a raindrop.

That once – you remember? – when you came up right next to me, just like that, out of the blue, when I least expected it. I kept my eyes averted just as you wished but I know you thought, 'If she can't stand with me, how will she lie with me?

And that shameful time I caught myself stroking my own arm, up and down, down and up, slowly, till I came to my senses and pretended I had a rash and they immediately changed the brand of joss sticks.

You follow me everywhere. On the terrace, in the kitchen, at prayer. You pull me by the hand, we run along like children down winding corridors, and then you stop by a pillar with chipped paint. The words you say are like letters written long, long ago.

I grow my hair at your behest. I had gotten used to it, you know, all the baldness. I used to like it even, the no-nonsense air it gave me, the air of authority among men. And now to the horror of those around me I start to grow my hair. I let it grow and grow. Past my ears, my neck, my shoulders, my waist, the small of my back, in Rapunzelian splendour, till loose or tied it is a being of its own.

I towel it dry sitting on the edge of my bed, head bent. You play with it, strand by strand, and I do nothing but ache, waiting for the moment I know you will cup the nape of my neck. My hair in your mouth, your mouth in my hair... I have licked my own hair, just to taste what you taste.

The earrings are sheer torture. When I asked my ears be pierced they called a meeting, a proper, formal meeting of many gray, ashen men who advised me against it. So I took a needle and did it myself and took real gold hoops off a gushing devotee. They weigh my earlobes down, the pierced skin yet to heal, but it's pleasure-pain, as well you know. You drag your gaze from wherever it is on me every time the hoop dances as I move my head.

I know you like me prim and proper, drinking my tea and reading the newspaper, till I come to bed at night that is, where the primmer I am, the madder you are. And the things you make me say! I can't even repeat them to myself.

Back in my room I ask to be left alone.

'Are you sick?' their eyes widen.

I eat the khichdi they so solicitously provide and count the minutes till they leave me alone and I can turn to you at last.

Yours, I whisper, all yours, nipple to navel to knee. And you come at me with a snarl, infuriated by your own lust. I surrender, a surrender mocked by the force of your embrace, its sheer taking. My clothes come off – the hands tugging at them mine, the urgency yours. First you push me into bed and explore me minutely, stroking a hip, lifting a thigh, squeezing, bruising, scratching with such blunt fingernails. You scoop my breasts in your hands and suckle both nipples at once, your cheeks flat with them.

You bend to where I pulse privately, secretly, deliciously. Gently, gently, I say, but there you go, all in a hurry. Your tongue tastes of tempests.

I look at you then, you are looking right back. And the silence, oh the silence, of not a word from you, not a word from me. If death took me now I would know not.

❦

The scandal hit me the hardest – naturally, since I was at the centre of it. It seems at a sponsored prayer meet for someone's dear departed I took off my clothes, every last binding bit of it, and plucking my plait free began to laugh, my sister miming me immediately, her laugh louder than mine. All efforts to control me were in vain. All efforts to re-clothe me, shush me, hide me away proved futile. I knew this and yet I did not know this. I could feel the pulls and pushes and above it all my mother's pleading scared voice calling me by a pet name. Which was when I narrowed my eyes at her; only *you* call me that.

I resisted all cries to come back, everyone was ready to believe my breakdown to be of a religious nature, that I stripped for God. But I couldn't lie. I took off my clothes for you. I wanted in those addled moments to flush you out of the great nowhere you are so fond of occupying, to make you visible, to no longer keep this phenomenal secret to myself but to gloat in all its glory, to have you by my side, to be part of a couple, a twosome, a pair, to be no longer alone. Yes, I knew why you came clandestinely, covertly, but, I was a girl after all, with a girl's heart, too carried away to realise how much this would damage you, how you could never come out and say it was you with me, me with you.

Many things struck terror in me as a child. The arrival of a music teacher twice a week every week, being cast alone in the storeroom during my menstrual times lest I contaminate, stray dogs at night... When I sit to think about it, almost every little thing used to frighten me, though none of these fears bore fruit, none of them actually played out till the end. They were instances of limited durations on a clock or calendar, of me shivering a bit and wanting to flee but in the end standing still meekly to go through whatever it was and being alive in the end.

In this ashram for abandoned women – an ashram built by me apparently, a me from the old days, as if I knew even then that I would need a place to end up in – I know I will never outrun the sheer, killing panic this time, the paralysing fear that this is it, we won't meet again, you and I, ever. That there will be no one at my deathbed, no you. That there will be everyone at your deathbed, no me. This I cannot think too long too much without falling into that endless groggy night from which I wake up with a broken-glass mouth and endless nightmares I never remember.

My matted hair I refuse to let them cut, to even touch. I woke up once to see them crouching over me with a pair of scissors and how I screamed and screamed.

I pass you by in corridors, you argue on the street below my window. Your voice, your laugh I can recognise anywhere. I hear, I hear every word you don't say to me. My eyes are shut, but I still see you, I always see you.

You sleep on my bed when I am not there. I enter rooms you've just exited. This, my punishment, I accept. Knowing you're near enough to touch, to smell, and the ungodly pain of it…

Every night I wait.

The Holy Sex Tape Project

MEENA KANDASAMY

THE NAÏVE MAY believe that the ban on porn can be bypassed if you know enough about the internet, how you get through using a proxy, about things like VPN and mirror-sites and torrent magnets and a million other things that involve some degree of technical expertise. But the ban that's in effect here, it's not just about asking some ISPs to block some meticulously prepared list of URLs. That's so old-school, and that's the kind of thing you do when you want to deflect attention from the lib-tards making a hue and cry about the falling rupee or the commies talking about their Teesta endlessly.

Now that there's an Indian man heading Google, and there's an Indian man heading Microsoft, and there's an Indian woman heading Pepsi, our authorities have come over their inferiority complexes and have (finally) learnt how to show the way ahead. They're in a different league now. No more the explicit, no more the dramatic. So, they've gone about doing it silently, as it should have been done long, long ago, deploying the testosterone-ridden rightwing army of the internet to look into every single website that has anything sexual in content. They merely have to report, and the video disappears. Is that a problem in itself? No. There's so much bad porn and snuff films and Western-peddled shit that I'd really wish they worked faster and took them all out. However, the actual problem is that these workers, sitting in front of their laptops all day, have developed a porn fatigue. Even as they probe into the underbelly of the internet, they are no longer able to distinguish between the everyday routine of an aunty lifting her legs in the most desultory fashion, and the grace of Urvashi ferris-wheeling over Indra. One is a boring voyeur video. The other is art and elegance and beauty, it's a dance of two bodies entwined in desire, it's a celebration of the fluidity of the female form, it's a choreography that seizes the viewer unawares and unprepared to take him on an unforgettable pleasure trip, it's a testimony to the heights of cultural refinement that we had reached as a civilisation. And it is important that we know the difference.

Why should a nice person like you be bothered about it? Not on a normal day, in a laidback world.

But the world is no longer what it was – a world where the word-of-mouth mattered more than what-you-see-is-what-you-get. Today, image is everything. Not the spoken word, not the printed page. Those who cannot understand the aesthetic argument of what I've just pointed out have to understand that our minds have been colonised. We have been taught by the invading Mughals and the British and the Christian missionaries that sex is haraam, bad, taboo, ugly. That is not the hallmark of the enlightened culture that we have always been before we were ruined by these foreigners. Sex in ancient India was celebrated. Courtesans were revered. Lovemaking was an art.

But when alien influences started seeping into our daily life, the ecstatic heights scaled by our ancestors were driven to the ground.

It is time that we revive our glorious heritage. It is time that we stand up against the commies, the pseudo-sickulars, the

Christian agents who talk against 'moral policing', not realising that we are an advanced civilisation when all of these people – Marx and Jesus and their forefathers – were still jumping from tree to tree. It is a time to act. It is time to act quickly and salvage what might be lost forever. In our immediate case, the millennia-old wisdom would become irretrievably lost not because of any external threat, but because our own enthusiastic young men (and women) who have been called to clean up the internet might mistakenly end up deleting some of the key episodes of passionate divine intercourse that have managed to survive to this day.

If you've watched only paid-Congi-media you are not going to buy into the belief that Shiva and Parvati actually made a sex tape of their interminable lovemaking. But it's true.

Vedic science was so evolved we actually launched satellites beyond the Andromeda to live-relay the ousting of dictators in distant planets there because we had already gotten to the stage of splendid democracy, we had achieved the division of labour and labourer through the caste system, and we were absolutely bored of what was happening on the local political scene. Plasma screens were passé, we were projecting things everywhere – over hot desert winds, over smelly sea breeze, over still air, over the flickering flames that shot up every time laser-sharp Sanskrit hymns were recited over the sacred fire. Back to this Shiva-Parvati episode – does it make sense that the dancing god stopped penetrating his lovely spouse because they wanted to save the universe, or prevent global warming, or because (as it is alleged) two others (Kama and Rati, though the Doniger woman might disagree) walked into the room? No. Shiva's longing and lust for Parvati is legendary. Even today we continue to worship the

symbol of their sexual union, the linga within a yoni, because of
the strong vibes that it emanates. Shiva's thrusts were so powerful
they shook the skies in seven parallel universes. Where Parvati's
nails dug into Shiva's back, little drops of blood trickled down
into the world, setting off volcanoes. They saw no shame in
their sensual urges. They were Indians, ffs. They were super-cool
about sex in public. This is where you have to put two and two
together – not in the sense of a foursome – and realise that the
coitus interruptus was because they were recording themselves
for posterity (the equivalent of today's homemade sex tapes),
and the presence of two others within their ultimate, divine
energy field was sure to ruin the amazing artwork that they
were creating. It would spoil their shared memory for eternity,
and the imprint of intruders into something so special would
leave anyone enraged, and finish up in great haste what must
have been otherwise, a long time coming.

Today's younger generation, as much tech-savvy as they
are, find it hard to believe that we had achieved these scientific
heights in our culture and civilisation. That's the sad side-
effect of four hundred years of the White Man's rule, and the
Macaulay-system of education that has made our young Indian
men and women into self-loathing creatures. Video technology,
broadband, wireless uploads, Bluetooth – what we see as the
innovations of the twenty-first century – were, in fact, already
obsolete in the Vedic era. Digital internet may be the path-
breaking development of this day and age, but we actually had
biological internet. Vedic scientist Gurudev Chaturvedi in his
seminal research work that combines wave theory, genetics and
hypercommunication has proved with concrete evidence, and
requisite Sanskrit etymology, that when hymns were chanted in

unison in hundreds of numbers, they created a powerful biological JavaScript-Enabled broadcast and invoked a communication with the DNA of those within the radius of influence of this sound and light energy. Moreover, the performance of yagnas with specific combustible material and in specific amounts produced the desired light energy which, when combined with these large organised chants and the filter coffee that was copiously ingested into every chanter, sent out massive broadcasting signals in the surrounding biological internet. Within the sphere of this biological internet, almost anything was possible.

A person could appear in two places, even ten thousand places at once. Our gods could copulate with a million apsaras at once, and drive each of them to an unforgettable climax. A divine being could transmogrify to take the shape that they preferred. At a particular frequency, a person could read the thoughts of others, by simply tuning into their minds. Transfer of data, of technology, of material was not done through physical matter, but *wirelessly*, through the supreme power of the scientific nature of our Sanskrit chants. In a situation like that, which existed during the Vedic times, memory itself became encapsulated and encrypted. No external storage was necessary, because everything could be accessed anytime, anywhere by those who had the asymmetric passkey. There was no limit on the data transfer. There was no fear of an Ashley-Madison style leak. A private moment, like the intense play of Krishna and Radha, was forever embedded in this multiverse. It remains tantalisingly hidden in plain sight.

The sceptics and Hindu-haters and self-appointed rationalists will now ask: How did this information enter the present-day internet? Those who have been thoroughly brainwashed by the mainstream media pressitutes may even buy this theory without understanding it through basic facts. Two facts have to be borne in mind. Firstly, the basics of quantum wave theory attest to the fact that every event exists as a 'wave function', which means that anything that has transpired has not been lost, but that the wave has merely travelled elsewhere. Secondly, remember that 36.5% of the NASA scientists are Indians, who have access to an incredible quantity of data. While a lot of it is rejected as junk or noise, one of the scientists, the illustrious late Parasuram Iyengar, set out working to de-encrypt these wave functions that were observed in outer space and stumbled upon this vast treasure trove of the carnal sublimations of our immortal gods. In the spirit of a true Hindu, he managed to convert these memory waves into something that our present-day technology can understand. In order to ward off suspicion from his activities, lest it be assumed by the repressed Westerners that he was watching salacious videos because they did not understand the true value of these episodes, he flooded the deep, hidden internet with them. He was awestruck by the beauty and glory of the divine lovemaking, but he unfortunately could not dedicate his life to spreading their glory to the Indians back home because he was called to work on the International Space Station from where he joined the astral universe. Today, as our young people sweep the internet in search of any available porn video and they arbitrarily remove them, they do not realise that they are destroying the rare gems that are our cultural inheritance.

That's why the *Holy Sex Tape Project* becomes a pressing necessity.

We require volunteers to find these videos, to share the URL on our database, to upload the video to our server, to rate the violence, to catalogue this information according to the number of protagonists, the nature of the sexual interaction, the list of positions adopted during the course of the intercourse, the presence of animal participants, the use of toys, and in addition, write out a hundred word description of the action that is taking place for the benefit of those who might want to browse through the synopsis before deciding which video to watch.

The thing is a lot of people would be reluctant about this kind of venture. After all, you are besieged everyday on Facebook and Twitter to sign a petition, support a cause, donate money, share an article, like a post, and convince yourself to feel guilty and responsible for everything that's wrong on this planet. This is not one of those mundane experiments.

In some of these sex tapes lie the greatest achievements of our civilisation. These tapes can simultaneously be the rite of passage for a young man at his *upanayana* ceremony; they can be the final farewell to an elder on his deathbed. This is a wealth of information that has lain buried and concealed as a secret, fearing foreign invasion and other threats. Now, it is no longer so.

And that is why we need you. We need your time. We have thirty-three million gods in our pantheon. Our gods are not repressed. Our gods saw the true beauty of the sensual; their pursuit of sexual play was to set an example to the human race. Remember, that these sexual acts were recorded not for the purposes of leisurely pastime, but to initiate and educate the future generations in the art of lovemaking. It's a lost art, but it has not been totally lost yet. By sharing this information, by making it accessible to the energetic Hindu youth, by preventing its mass elimination, you will render a great service to our society.

For those of you who feel that you might, at some point in

the near future, qualify to become a volunteer for the project but are held back because of prudery, remember that it is because you have been conditioned against sex as a result of your convent, Catholic education. Notwithstanding your own opinions, you must partake in this noble quest not only to appreciate the advances that our civilisation and our religion has made in the realm of the carnal and the spiritual, but also because it is your patriotic duty at this moment of crisis. You must step forward and volunteer in this ambitious project because our motherland now stands at an hour of peril. For the first time in the history of Bharatavarsha, Hindus are no longer eighty percent of the population. The numbers are on a downward slide. The numbers show that we have given up desire; we have given up our duty of procreation. Our women no longer have the fertile wombs that graced our foremothers. Their thighs no longer hold the same unquenchable hungers, their yonis no longer ache for the soothing pleasures of sex, they no longer take pride in the triumphant swollen belly that heralds their motherhood. It is not just our women who have let us down. Our men were once proud stallions. Their reputation relied on their capacity to please. They could denude a woman with a piercing look. They knew the art of sex. They could leave their lover throbbing with desire, pleading for time to still itself. They saw no shame in copulation. They were driven by lust, they took any woman who fancied them, and sowed their wild oats everywhere. Today, they have been emasculated publicly. They have forgotten who they were. They have forgotten their duty to procreate. Soon we will be a lost tribe waiting to be discovered by a Discovery channel crew from Guatemala.

Our decimation caused by our disinterest in sex must stop.

Now the remedy is at hand. The sultry eyes of Indrani, the quivering lips of Shakuntala, the honey skin of Chitrasena, the hollow cheekbones of Aditi, the slender shoulder-blades of Menaka, the arrogant breasts of Tilottama, the large nipples of Sulochana, the slim waist of Ahalya, the alluring navel of Madhura, the heavy hips of Sunanda, the eager, dextrous fingers of Rambha, the never-ending legs of Shakti, the interlocking embrace of Kamya, the conch-shell yoni of Tara, the arched dancing feet of Ambika, the miraculous flexibility of Anjana as she folds herself over her lover, all these are destined to spice up your love-life and ignite your endless desire.

This is not a male domain. There is plenty of fare for our sisters too. The engorged, tireless lingas of our divine immortals will allow you to relish the virility and masculinity of our men, and save you from the perils of being lured into the love jihad that is being unleashed in every street corner.

Remember, the true test of the aesthetics of erotica is its ability to cause arousal. In the journey you are about to embark upon, in the material that will be made available for your viewing pleasure, there is no shortage of the heights of passion that you can reach.

There are other aspects of your personality that will undoubtedly gain from your selfless devotion to the task at hand. Like the five Pandava brothers, you will hone five different skills that will keep you in good stead.

Like Yudhistra, you will learn to stick to the just cause; you will not be deviated in your pursuit of the same. Others might deride you for spending hours in front of your computer. Ignore them, for they are not aware. What you are doing is a service to our society, and any amount of nay-saying and disheartening comments from others should dissuade you from the task at hand.

Like Bheema, who fathered Hidimbi's son Ghatotkatcha, you will learn to appreciate the beauty of the other races. Even as you remain a proud Aryan, you will develop a fascination for the dark-skinned Dravidian women of the South, the petite women of the hills, the varied women of the faraway lands. Never forget that Golwalkar, the Supreme Leader of our organisation, pointed out that experiments in cross-breeding were carried out by our forefathers in an effort to better the human race. It was the Aryans, the Brahamanas of North India who settled in the South and impregnated the women there. You will be driven not by carnal lust alone – for who cannot be swayed by the generous hips of the Malabar women – but by the desire to spread the power of your superior race.

Like Arjuna, you will learn to maintain your focus. He managed to shoot the eye of a fish looking at its reflection in the water in a palace surrounded by a thousand spectators. Likewise, you will learn to harness your energies and pull yourself together as you complete the job. Even as your own body betrays you by succumbing to the capricious charm of a Yakshini's copious breasts, even as you cannot resist the temptation of climaxing yourself, even as a certain wetness wells up within you, you will concentrate on the task at hand, putting information in all the right boxes, subtly learning all the tricks of the trade, but never losing your focus.

Like handsome Nakula, you will learn to appreciate your own good looks. Once the greatest race to have walked the earth, our men today are riddled with shyness, with awkwardness, they are unsure of their place in the world. The Hindu man has lost the dashing aggression that once characterised him. You will remember that you are a warrior, a hero, full of muscular strength and sexual stamina.

Like Sahadeva, the most intelligent man who ever walked this earth, you will learn the power of silence. Sahadeva, entreated by his dying father to eat his burnt flesh, obeyed the command and acquired the power to foresee the past, the future, and the ripple effect of all our actions. And yet, when asked by others to reveal what he knew, he maintained a steady silence. Such a silence is required in today's world. Lesser mortals will not understand the universes that are destroyed in the death-grip of a yoni, they will not understand the temporary moksha of riding a woman in the reclining lotus position. That is a knowledge to which only you, and the select few like you, can have access. When asked by anyone who does not believe in our cause, silence shall be your most powerful weapon. You are not obliged to share your ecstasy with those who are traitors to our religion.

In a sense, this altruistic act of volunteering with the *Holy Sex Tape Project* will benefit you in every sphere of your life. The joys are too numerous to be listed, and the modesty of this author prevents him from spelling out things in greater, explicit detail.

And finally, do not forget the best advantage of being a volunteer: You'll know how to please your partner day after day. There'll never be a boring night. This could change your life. This will change the world. Sign up now. Spread the word. Please visit http://www.holysextapeproject.in to register. Let us save the last remnants of our glorious past and our unparalleled culture before it is too late.

Graveyard Shift

KANKANA BASU

ANU STOOD GAZING into the mirror. Sunlight had receded outside. A blanket of darkness was descending on the city. The lights had not yet been switched on, and the room was shadowy in the gathering dusk. The reflection in the mirror was swathed in a lavender-hued mist, lending it an aura of mystery.

'Anu. Ugh! What a ghastly plebian name. I should have some other name, something enigmatic, sexy, unforgettable – Marylene, Greta, Tanya, Kamini – a hot name for a hot bod. Razia, Shabnam, Rosy…' Anu made direct conversation with the image in the mirror. 'Shabnam, hmm… Shabnam sounds good. Reminds me of the cabaret dancer in that old film *Kati Patang*, gyrating and teasing the poor heroine, mera naam hai Shabnam, pyaar se mujhe log Shabbo kehte hain… Perfect, just perfect! For now, I'm going to be Shabnam. Shabnam!'

Shabnam lifted a bare arm and ran dainty fingers through her rich dark hair. She tossed her head to one side, giving her mane a fashionably tousled look. Twisting with languid grace, she thrust her breasts forward and crossed her thighs, striking a Khajuraho-style pose before the mirror. Excitement surged through her loins. It was time to get moving.

Opening her wardrobe, she chose a clingy glittering top in black that showed off her pert breasts to perfection. Next came

a long chiffon skirt in midnight blue slit down the side; her
left leg, she knew, would flash tantalisingly as she walked. She
pirouetted before the mirror for a few moments, then sprayed
herself liberally with perfume, picked up a handbag and stepped
out.

The house, a rambling one-storey affair inherited from
her grandfather, was a solitary structure huddled under an old
banyan tree. It had narrowly missed being demolished by the
municipal authorities when the road was widened. A roughly
hewn rock idol of the monkey-god Hanuman stood at the
base of the banyan tree, attracting the occasional devotee. The
authorities, not wanting to cause a religious controversy, had
thought it wise to leave that particular patch of land alone.
Which suited Shabnam just fine. The large dilapidated house
with a rundown garden stood isolated, and there was no one
to witness the frequency of her nocturnal departures. She'd have
a drink at a bar and head towards Byculla station later in the
night, she decided, as she sashayed along.

Shabnam's heels clicked rhythmically on the pavement. Few people
were out at this late hour. Women were hardly visible, except for
a couple of call-centre girls tumbling sleepily out of a car or the
odd air-hostess decked up in flying gear waiting for the airline
van to pick her up. The building watchmen hovered solicitously
around these air hostesses whenever they reported for duty late
in the night, Shabnam noticed, and their protective air evoked
deep amusement in her. The bastards, she muttered to herself.
She was sure the paternal attitude of these men in uniform was
phony. Under the proprietorial manner lurked baser instincts.

A couple of roadside Romeos, typical inhabitants of Mumbai's by lanes, stood leaning against a paan-bidi kiosk and one of them let out a low wolf whistle as Shabnam clicked past. She ignored them. She was not in a mood for group activities of the amorous kind. Today, she felt the need for a passionate one-on-one encounter.

She took the narrow abandoned track that ended just behind a railway platform. The man was coming towards her, swaying drunkenly, and she spotted him before he saw her. They were heading in opposite directions, drawing closer to each other. She knew what his next move would be; she had watched him and others like him in action with other women many a time in the past. He'd lurch when he came alongside and his hand would brush her thigh.

It happened exactly as she had anticipated. But unlike what his victims typically did, she did not screech, slap, punch or ignore his lecherous hand snaking up the slit in her skirt. Instead, she gave him a sidelong inviting smile. The drunk did a double take. Was this divine-smelling memsaab-type actually giving *him* come-hither signals?

He had lucked out, lucked out in the most mother-fucking way! Holding him by the hand and smiling coquettishly, Shabnam led him to the corner of the abandoned yard that was now stacked with sacks of potatoes waiting to be transported some place. Nobody ever came this way after dark, and it was the perfect setting for a romantic rendezvous. The drunk followed her in a bemused fashion. Shabnam lifted a hand and brushed her fingertips over the man's thick slobbering lips and heard his breath catch in his throat.

The next moment, they had tumbled down over the potato

sacks in unison holding on to each other and she could hear him
breathing noisily as he began undressing her with unsteady hands.
She lay back and, arching her body, thrust herself provocatively
into him, all the while wondering how far he'd go. The stark
contrast in the nature of their bodies and bodily scents created
a sense of euphoria deep within her. She suspected that this
play of contrasts gave her more pleasure than the actual act of
lovemaking. Or the chosen lover of the night…. The headlong
clash between Elizabeth Arden and cheap booze, Victoria's
Secret crushed against stale sweat, soft skin against rough hairy
limbs…. She purposely writhed and twisted under him, teasing
him further. The man uttered an obscenity and suddenly turned
rough. He pinned her down, and she could hear the sucking and
gobbling motions of his mouth at her breasts. His pelvis was
coming down on hers and she half-turned to her side quickly.
Unable to hold on any longer, he started rubbing and thrusting
in a frenzy against her naked thigh, his tempo increasing rapidly.
There was grating, sighing, and moaning in the deserted yard,
stinking skin against velvet limbs, expensive lingerie ripping
under calloused hands, the fusing of foreign perfume with the
smells of unwashed underwear and hooch. Would he go all the
way, she wondered suddenly, worried. She'd have to think of a
way to stop him… how far would the blighter actually go? Not
too far, she discovered in mild relief. In the throes of passion
and unable to hold on any more, he came all over her exposed
thigh. She could feel the warm stickiness on her freshly epilated
skin. For a moment she lay still, trying to savour the moment
and all it contained; satiation on one side, frustration as well as
relief on the other; chauvinism, selfishness, and the familiar old
frustration of not being able to climax after a spot of inspired

foreplay. Some moments came so heavily charged with meaning and emotion and paradoxes, she revelled in them, actually. They were like a heavily pregnant woman about to go into labour, these potent moments that came by so rarely, mused Shabnam, in an oddly dreamy state now. But they more than made up for the barren days that preceded and followed them.

It was all over for tonight, however. She let out a low guttural moan and heaved the man off her supine body.

White hot anger raged through her the next minute. Her usual mood swing was setting in. A fiery hatred for the male species blinded her. This was the usual drill with her. A flirtation followed by passion followed by orgasmic bliss followed by uncontrollable rage. The sequence was always the same. Why were men such beasts, she growled to herself. Why were they such selfish bastards who could only think of their own pleasure? Once they were done, they had no qualms about throwing aside lovers still in the middle of unfinished climaxes... Beasts!

Shabnam stood up, straightening her dress in sharp angry strokes. She walked away from the man in brisk steps, heading for the over bridge that ran over all the platforms. A slant-eyed glance back at the man was met with by a bored, leery look. What use was a woman, even a fancy upmarket bitch, once the act was over, his expression seemed to say. She felt combustible, capable of exploding into flames any minute.

She trudged up the over bridge feeling heavy and disoriented. Reaching the top, she stood quietly, holding on to the railings. The railway tracks lay dark and silent below her. She took in large noisy gulps of the cool night air.

The tracks gleamed dully in the deficient moonlight. As she stood watching, a gigantic golden glow seemed to light up a point on the horizon. The glow turned steadily brighter, and the scene below changed dramatically. Gone were the untidy boxes of wires, the mounds of human excreta dropped from long distance trains and rats scurrying around in the darkness. In the golden headlights of the approaching train, the filthy railway stretch appeared to morph into a land of indescribable beauty, a terrain of fantasy capable of delivering infinite promises.

The drunk was trudging up the over bridge steps, the belt at his waist still loose, his fly open. Turning slowly towards him, Shabnam crooked a finger, summoning him. He came stumbling awkwardly, still in the grip of a post-coital daze. She watched him approach. Shabnam had had her fill of sweat, saliva and semen for the night (she touched her sticky skirt fleetingly), she needed to taste one other bodily fluid urgently: blood.

She beckoned to the man to come closer and he came and stood beside her at the railing. He was breathing noisily. The stench from his body overwhelmed her. A sudden feeling of repugnance made her want to throw up. She stretched out a naked arm, indicating the gold-lit scene below them.

'Look down, lover-boy,' she whispered.

He gazed down obediently.

'Look long and hard. Your glimpse of paradise. Who can say, but you may never again know a night such as this.'

The man squinted down in perplexity, shoving his head far over the railing. The smell of urine and hot asphalt wafted into the night air.

Shabnam's hand snaked out and clamped over the back of the drunk's neck. He nearly let out an astonished roar but Shabnam, a practiced hand, was quick. With surprising strength she drove his head downwards with one hand. Hooking the fingers of her other hand into his trouser's waist band, she snarled an oath and heaved his body over the railing. The man went spinning down, his shrill scream of terror was muted by the deafening horn of a passenger train as it came charging towards the over bridge and thundered past.

When all was quiet, Shabnam peered down. The broken body of the man lay on the tracks, his limbs askew.

'Number six,' she muttered with quiet satisfaction and dusted her hands.

Mopping at the sticky slit of the skirt and gathering up her disheveled hair, she raced down the steps. She had to get out of the station before anyone spotted her or the body on the tracks. Outside, a Sikh taxi driver slumbered at his wheel. Shabnam slid into the rear seat silently.

She slept late and was woken up by the sound of the garden gate opening. The rusty hinges that needed oiling and the gate let out its usual protesting groan when pushed. Anu looked at the clock. Eleven o' clock! She had slept all through the morning! The previous night's escapade came back to her and she felt a rush of pure pleasure. What a night! She was done being Shabnam, however. Tonight she would be Tanya, or Rosy, or any of those exotic sounding women whom men lusted over. Every other night would bring fresh excitement, she promised herself, and a new identity would be carefully constructed; she was a restless soul forever in a state of transmogrification.

'I could tell you my adventures from this evening but it's no use going back to yesterday, because I was a different person then,' she said aloud, softly, to herself. That's what Alice had said to the Mock Turtle.

Then she laughed, and couldn't stop laughing. She had been reading *Alice in Wonderland* aloud to her students just yesterday, discussing the illusory nature of the book. An instant later, in a strangely random manner, memories of a childhood summer had flooded her mind. A summer of growing up overnight, of mixed identities, gender confusion, and an unbearable pain. A big group of grown-ups – her parents, her aunts and uncles, and all her cousins had gone to a seaside resort, she recalled, now fairly detached about the entire episode, and the large bunch of kids (which included her, the youngest) had been entrusted to the care of a man-servant. Kaleidoscopic images spun around in her mind – of endless walks taken on damp beaches, sand castles built meticulously only to be demolished by devilish older cousins, ice lollies in rainbow hues, sea breeze in the hair, swimming in emerald waters...

And then, the hairy hands, the underwater groping, the pain, the shame, the ecstasy. The man-servant had walked away nonchalantly, whistling, fondling his crotch. She never spoke about the servant or what he did to her but had begun to hate anything and everything to do with hairy limbs and male genitals. Anything that had even a fleeting phallic resemblance had to go. Any man who aroused her had to go. Men with hairy hands had to go. Any man who took her for granted after sex had to go.

She rose and made her way to the window to check who was calling on her at this unusual hour. What a pity Dhan Bahadur, her Nepali watchman, was not there anymore. He had kept a strict vigil and screened visitors for her. She remembered with pleasure the sinewy arms of the young Nepali, the smell of onions in his armpits, and his tendency to ejaculate prematurely. She could still feel the pressure of his squat body crushing her fragile frame as they tumbled about on the very sofa she'd been lying on a minute ago. Such a pity, she sighed, that DB had to go. Just like number two and three, and the others. It all had to do with bad timing, putrid memories and missed moments, really.

It was the postman at the gate. He was talking to somebody on the street. He would soon step into the compound and head for her front door. In his other hand, the man held a pale green official-looking envelope and her heart leapt with joy. Her passport had arrived! How eagerly she had been waiting for it. She had suffered severe anxiety pangs at the delay, for it was well past three months since she'd applied. The police checking had also come with its share of uneasy moments; she was not the glib liar she had imagined herself to be and had fumbled with her answers. But now her passport had arrived! Thank god. She really needed to get out of the country, and stay out for a while. Visit her siblings in New Zealand, maybe. Spend time away from home till things calmed down a bit. The school where she taught English to seventh graders would be closing for summer vacations soon in any case. Even as alarm bells rang in her head she was itching to take the score to number seven, or maybe more.

Anu moved languidly. Loosening the waistband of her skirt, she let it drop. It fell in a neat circle and she stepped out of it nimbly. Picking up a pair of track pants draped untidily around a chair, she pulled them on. Raising her arms, she peeled off the glittering top and unhooked her heavily padded bra. Topless, she sauntered over to the wardrobe in search of a T-shirt, her fingers playing with the small triangle of hair on her chest. She pulled at the first thing that came to her hand – an old grey jersey. Her fingers plucked at her hairline next, and in one swift movement she pulled off the luxuriant wig. Pink scalp showed beneath it, covered in scant hair. Picking up a pair of reading glasses, she slid them on.

The doorbell rang. There was no cause for concern; she was ready to receive visitors. A peek through the eye-hole in the door revealed the oily paan-chewing face of the postman who always came with official documents. There was a disgruntled look on his face. He knew no bakshish could be expected at this address. So true, so very true, thought Anu, grinning to herself. She was damned if she was going to shell out money for what was rightfully hers.

The door opened and the postman found himself staring at the balding bookish face of the man who never gave tips.

'Mr Anupam Bhagat?' he said, with forced politeness. 'Your passport has arrived, sir. May I have some sort of proof of your identity?'

First Kiss

VIKRAM KAPUR

IT WAS 1981. I was thirteen. The greatest discovery I had made since becoming a teenager was that it changed nothing. I remained the sorry self I was at twelve, in fact even sorrier as you will soon learn, and the same could be said for the world around me. When I look back now, I guess the banality of turning thirteen prepared me for the banality of other birthdays that are supposed to rock your world – sixteen, eighteen, twenty-one… I met them all with suitably low expectations.

The abiding memory I have of thirteen is of standing in front of my bathroom mirror. Each night I would park myself there and study my nakedness. It was a challenge, since the mirror was made to gaze at faces. To fit in anything below the chest I had to stand on tip-toe. When it came to below the waist, I had to go get a stool.

Still, I went through the routine of studying parts of myself night after night. The skinny arms, the skinny legs, the skinny chest… Those I had known for years. There was another skinny part of which I had become painfully aware only recently thanks to my only friend, Pinky Sethi. One day, while munching on tiffin during a break in the quad at Delhi Public School, he whispered, You know girls like big dicks. He had read that in some book. The first thing I did after imbibing that pearl of wisdom was to examine my dick as soon as possible. What I saw gutted me. Not only was it small, it was downright scrawny.

I had no idea then that the only kind of dick that matters in sex is an erect dick. (Mine, when erect, became much fuller and longer.) Pinky didn't tell me that; he probably had no idea either. Messrs Harold Robbins and James Hadley Chase, whose books I smuggled into the house to devour in the bathroom or when my parents were out, also omitted that piece of information while describing sex. A footnote that read something like – all the dicks described here are erect – would have helped mightily. There was no internet or Google at the time for me to find out all there was to know about dicks. And there was no way I could discuss my problem with anyone. In the India of the eighties, there was no dirtier word than sex. We just didn't have sex then; we had children. I can't even imagine the hell in which I would have descended if I had tried to discuss my problem with my parents. Hey, Mummy, Daddy, can we talk about my dick today? My only sibling was my brother Vinay, an electrical engineer, who was twelve years older than me and working in Boston. Given the difference in age, I doubt if Bhaiya's reaction would have been any different from that of my parents. He saw me as his baby brother and babies aren't exactly supposed to think of dick sizes. And there was no way I was going to breathe a word about it to my peers, even Pinky. Hey, you know I got a small, skinny one. No way.

It was really my dick that put me in front of that mirror every night. I guess I was hoping for a miracle. Each night I'd get up on that stool and examine it from every possible angle, before measuring its length and breadth with a ruler. Each night it insisted on remaining its old sorry self. I was used to the rest of my skinniness; I had lived with it for years. The dick was a fresh cut, one that promised to bleed for the rest of my life. There was hope in the gym for my skinny legs, arms and chest. But where on earth was the gym that could puff up a dick?

The rest of my skinny self had already played havoc with my self-esteem. My dick sent it plunging through the basement. Forget about asking a girl out, I was too ashamed to look one in the eye. I observed them from afar with the eyes of an ardent fan devouring his favourite movie star. Thin girls, fat girls, lovely girls, ugly girls… All the girls I had known or would come to know had been rendered unattainable. It seemed the only sex life available to me was that of a voyeur.

Pinky was in the same boat. If my problem was skinniness, his was bulk. (I'm not talking about his dick here; I have no idea how big or small that is.) He looked like he carried two footballs in his stomach to go with a tennis ball in his mouth. His cheeks were not only bloated, they were so red that I often wondered if he had spilled his mother's blush-on all over them. When he laughed, his small eyes disappeared from sight and all you could see of his face was a lot of buck teeth sticking out of a wad of red flesh.

I guess we were a latter-day Laurel and Hardy. We certainly got a lot of laughs, though not because we were funny. We were just plain sad.

That we were probably closer to Mars than a snog didn't prevent us from talking about sex. To tell the truth, no matter where our conversation began that was where it ended up. Our frame of reference was the novels we read. Porn magazines were hard to obtain and well beyond the reach of our pocket money. The only way we could ever watch a porn film was to smuggle the video cassette into the house and view it on the family VCR when the rest of the family was out. That wasn't feasible at thirteen; our parents considered us far too young to be left alone.

That Sunday I was lounging in the divan in my drawing room in my kurta-pyjama and watching the India-Pakistan Test match on our black and white television. The phone rang in the lobby and my mother informed me that Pinky was calling. I went over to where the black phone squatted on a wooden stand. 'Hi, Pinky, what are you doing, man?' I intoned into the receiver.

There was a short pause before he said, 'I started reading this book last night.'

His voice had dropped to a whisper. My heart quickened. If Pinky wanted to talk about a book in such hushed tones, it had to be positively filthy.

'There's a scene in there, yaar, I read it again and again but even then mine wouldn't sit.'

I swallowed. 'So it's required reading,' I said.

We reviewed the books we read as required reading or not; an early sign that we'd grow up to be teachers.

'Definitely required,' Pinky said.

'What's this book?' I asked.

'*The Godfather*. It's by Mario Puzo.' His voice dropped further as he added, 'You have to look at page twenty-seven.'

The movie version of *The Godfather* had been passed For Adults Only by the censors. The book's notoriety rose even further in my eyes.

Pinky was keen to talk more. I couldn't wait to get off the phone and run to the lending library in the neighbourhood market to dive into *The Godfather*. In those days we lived in

Defence Colony and the market was a short walk from my home. I ended the conversation quickly and said goodbye.

I ran out of the house, forgetting to close the front gate in my haste. Since it was a Sunday, the traffic was virtually nonexistent. All I encountered on my way was a cyclist. Normally, it took ten minutes. That day I made it in eight minutes flat. The market was two lines of shops facing each other across a small park and a couple of narrow, one-way streets going in opposite directions. In my haste, I looked the wrong way while crossing them and was reminded of my mistake by a furious horn.

The library was located at one end of the market. It was actually a cramped, secondhand bookshop called Love, Laugh and Learn (or the 3Ls) that rented out books and magazines for a fee. The books were crammed in the shelves built in the walls, as well as in the large bookcase that loomed like a partition in the middle of the shop. The latest issues of the magazines hung just above head height on a clothesline across the front of the shop. They were held up by clothes pegs. You passed the counter on the way in.

I groaned the moment I entered the shop.

For the past six months, the bookshop had been manned by its owner Mr Vij's young nephew Suresh. That day Suresh was nowhere to be seen. Old man Vij was at the counter.

Mr Vij was everything that Suresh was not. Well into his sixties, he was far too removed from his teens to have any sympathy for a teenager's hormones. Suresh was only twenty-two and retained some memory of what it had been like to be a teenager. Worse, Mr Vij, unlike Suresh, knew my parents well. With him I was sure that news of my reading a dirty book would get back to them.

'Good morning, Anil,' Mr Vij said.

'Good morning, Uncle.' I doubt if I've ever sounded more mournful while wishing someone good morning. I'd already spotted the book on the shelf reserved for authors whose last name began with P. I was itching to get my hands on it. Mr Vij's presence, however, guaranteed that wasn't going to happen any time soon. I'd be pulling the book out in front of his eyes.

Then providence stepped in. Mrs Nayar breezed into the shop.

A plump, bespectacled schoolteacher in her forties, she was known for her voracious appetite for books. She stepped up to the counter and quizzed Mr Vij about the latest offerings. Mr Vij forgot about me as he tried to parry her questions. That was the opportunity I needed to duck behind the bookcase with *The Godfather*. Feverishly, I flipped to page twenty-seven and started devouring the goings-on between Sonny Corleone and Lucy Mancini. As I read, my breathing grew laboured and my mouth went dry.

'Oh, my god,' a girl's voice sounded.

My eyes rose from the page to rest on a girl in her mid-teens squatting on the floor next to the bookcase. She was staring at the front of my pyjama.

Had I been wearing a kurta-pyjama that fitted me, I would have been spared that moment. The one I had on was way too small. Last night I had been in a situation where my nightclothes were either dirty or with the dhobi who hadn't come for a week. So I was forced to wear a kurta-pyjama that I had outgrown. It was a little longer than a pair of bermuda shorts and the kurta, instead of dropping down to my knees, ended at my waist, leaving the erection plainly visible. Not just that, there was a dark, wet stain spreading on the fabric.

The Godfather fell from my hands. My only thought now was to get away from there as fast as possible. Shielding the stain with clasped hands, I stepped out from behind the bookcase. Leaving a wide-eyed Mr Vij staring after me, I brushed past Mrs Nayar and ran out into the street.

What happened in that bookshop should have cured me of fretting about my dick for the rest of my life. After all, I had been noticed because of its size. A shrivelled member would have rested anonymously in my pajamas and I would have passed through that girl's life unnoticed. Now she was sure to remember me, thanks to my dick.

Alas, I missed the point altogether. In the days that followed, the very thought of that moment made me want to hide. In the past, I had badmouthed my dick for not growing. Now I castigated it for having grown. The girl, instead of being living proof of the fact that I had nothing to fear in terms of dick size, became the fountainhead of my embarrassment. The idea of running into her again made me want to disappear down a hole. I didn't leave the house for days, except to go to school, and I would have bunked school every day if it weren't for my parents.

My mother couldn't figure it out. Why have you gone into purdah? she kept asking. I expected to bump into that girl the moment I stepped out of my front gate, which made me jumpy every time I left the house. In school I had the furtive eyes of a fugitive. Pinky bore with me for a few days before asking, 'Did you kill someone?'

It was a month before I started shedding my purdah. It wasn't that I was any less scared; I was quaking the first time I went back to the bookshop. It was just that I was bored silly after being a purdahnasheen for so long. To my relief that first trip to the bookshop was uneventful. Mr Vij muttered a distracted hello. The girl was nowhere to be seen. After that, things became easier as the memory grew more remote and the girl failed to materialise.

Two months after the bookshop incident, my brother sent a letter from America that made my parents whoop with delight. They had been working on him for a year to get married. In that letter, he finally said yes.

I don't think a pot of gold would have made my parents happier. They went about the house like a pair of light-footed children. My mother visited the temple to break a coconut. My father went around telling anyone who'd listen, I knew it, I knew it. He'd never marry a mem. He's my son.

I watched them, growing more amazed by the minute. For the life of me I couldn't figure out why Bhaiya wanted to get married. As far as I was concerned, the only reason to get married was to have sex. There was simply no other way to get it in India in the eighties. No other way that gelled with middle-class morality that is. But Bhaiya was no longer in India. He was in America where it rained beautiful women and having sex was as routine as drinking Coca Cola. Or so I thought. Furthermore, I couldn't figure out why he was letting our parents choose the woman he was going to fuck for the rest of his life. At least he could trust his own dick on that count.

When Bhaiya arrived, he did nothing to dispel my bemusement. Rather, he added to it by speaking as little as possible. He had been quiet before he went to America a year ago. He came back quieter. I was dying for stories of fast cars, fast women and Hollywood. That is how I saw America in those days. All I got from my brother were statements that went something like *I have been far too busy to do anything or go anywhere.* Listening to them, I wondered whether he had spent the past year in America or in a sweatshop. What was more, he didn't want to go out anywhere; it's far too hot, he kept saying, his brows knitted. He spent most of his time in his room, appearing only for meals that he ate in silence. I thought he had turned into a piece of dead wire badly in need of an electric charge. The only time he seemed to acquire a few amperes was when he was watching baseball. He had brought back videocassettes of Boston Red Sox games that he kept replaying night after night. He knew how things would pan out in each game; yet he devoured them as if he was watching a highly anticipated final live.

If my parents were concerned about how an Indian girl would deal with my brother's newfound love for baseball, they didn't show it. They went ahead full throttle with their plan of finding him a wife. Less than a week after he touched down in Delhi, an ad was placed in the matrimonial section of the Sunday newspaper. The first requirement for a prospective bride was for her to be fair. I read that and wondered why my father had been so concerned about Bhaiya marrying a mem. Who could be fairer than a white woman?

By next week, the resumes of prospective brides were pouring in. My parents scrutinised them and prepared a shortlist, after which they set up meetings with the women and their families. One morning I was informed that we were going to see a girl in the tony neigbourhood of Jor Bagh.

The girl was a thin-jawed woman, with a narrow face and pointed nose, who had just graduated from Lady Shri Ram

College. She was quite attractive in her picture. My parents, though, were more taken by her father who was an I.AS. officer and owned a large house in a posh neighbourhood. They are khandaani people, my father kept saying. If Bhaiya had an opinion on the matter, he didn't air it.

The house in Jor Bagh was a single-storey kothi with a garage, a garden, and servant quarters. The father met us at the front door. He was a slim man of average height who would have been nondescript if it weren't for the bald patch in the middle of his head that looked like Sri Lanka with an Indian Ocean of white hair flowing round it. Even in the forty-degree heat he was wearing a double-breasted suit. He escorted us into a large drawing room with a TV, two plush sofas, a divan, a Persian carpet, and walls containing several paintings and family portraits. The mother and two daughters were waiting there.

I froze the moment I saw the younger girl. The heat rose in my cheeks, my chest and stomach tightened, and I was beset with an urge to flee.

It was *her*.

Her name was Maya. She was sixteen, and the first thing she did when she saw me was exclaim, 'You're the boy from the bookshop!'

Her lips were pressed together. She was desperately trying to quench the laughter spreading inside her like wildfire. It had already lit up her eyes and was causing her chest and shoulders to writhe. In the end, it spilled out of her and enveloped me in a flame of embarrassment. My cheeks felt like they'd been placed on hot coals. I was sure they had grown reddish-pink, like pieces of tandoori chicken fished out of a tandoor. The tips of my ears were on fire.

Everyone else seemed bemused. I'm sure they could see the 'meeting' in the bookshop had been no ordinary meeting. But they had congregated there with matchmaking in mind and were not going to let a couple of hysterical teenagers who were marginal to the entire process get in the way. 'Maya, why don't you show Anil your room?' her mother said. The expression on her face screamed, 'Get the hell out of here'. Maya, who obviously knew that look well, rose with her mouth still full of laughter. My mother gave me a glance that pretty much cloned the one on Maya's mother's face. I had no wish to go with Maya. But I had no choice. Reluctantly, I followed her to her room.

Her room was on the other side of the house. It was a mess with books piled up on the desk and clothes thrown all over a chair. A bookcase blocked one wall. Posters of pop singers blanketed the other three. A bed with a dark-brown bedcover sprawled in the middle.

I stood just inside her door, unable to meet her eyes.

'I'm sorry but I just couldn't get over the sight of you running out of that bookshop,' she said. Her voice was deep and throaty, unlike any other girl I knew. Still deeply embarrassed, I shuffled about with my eyes lowered.

A few tortuous seconds passed before she said, 'Please sit down.'

There was no place to sit other than the bed. I settled on its edge. She sat down next to me. The moment she did, my knees slapped together.

'You can relax,' she said.

She smelled of freshly cut jasmine flowers. I remained as tight as ever with my hands clasped, my body rigid and my knees glued together.

'It's okay,' she said. Her voice was lower and huskier. Her fingers gently slid over the veins on my wrist. As she continued to caress them, a tingle ran up my arm. The knots tying up my body began to fall away. My hands unclasped. My knees parted. A shudder raced through my back.

I turned to look at her properly for the first time. She was about my height and dressed in a pair of jeans and a black sleeveless T-shirt. She had skin the colour of old ivory. Her face was almost an oval with a cleft on the chin. Her lips were lightly touched up with red lipstick. Her shoulder-length hair was combed forwards on to her forehead, so that her eyes seemed to stare out from the mouth of a cave. They were lovely eyes, the colour of almonds, and twice as big as mine. Right now they were shining in a way I had never seen a pair of eyes shine before. The outline of her bra was visible below the T-shirt. In my head, I could see the breasts underneath; melon-like breasts with a perfect set of erect brown nipples. I swallowed hard, as my dick came alive in my pants. I ached to throw my arms around her; to crush her against me and kiss her all over her face and body. But I was afraid. I had never touched a girl with desire. I remained where I was. She was the one who finally leaned forward. Her lips brushed against mine and her tongue slid over my mouth. I was too taken aback to respond. She drew back, glaring.

'Why don't you open your mouth?' she said.

I had no idea what she was talking about. I gazed dumbly at her. Her eyes narrowed. 'Do you know what a French kiss is?'

I had read enough to know what it entailed but had no idea what it was called. I shook my head. Her eyes opened wide. 'How old are you?'

It did not occur to me to lie. 'Thirteen,' I said.

'What?' She leaped off the bed as if stung. 'Thirteen, my god.' Her hands flew to her head. 'The size of that dick – I thought he was at least fifteen. Thirteen!'

She paced up and down the room, hands on her head. I watched her, stupefied by what had transpired. Suddenly, she stopped pacing and launched into a rant. I was to blame for everything that had happened. I should have told her I was thirteen. If she'd known she would never have acted the way she did. It was as if I had tricked her into it. Grabbing my shoulders, she told me not to breathe a word of it to anyone. If I did she'd make sure the wrath of god came down upon me.

I don't know how long she would have gone on if it weren't for the knock on the door; a servant asking us to come because the meeting was over and my family was ready to leave.

I left the house in a daze. I don't remember anything about the rest of the day. All I could see or hear was Maya in her various incarnations. The laughing Maya, the ranting Maya, the seductive Maya… It was only at night that things changed. Maya's other incarnations vanished, to leave me snuggling in bed with the seductive Maya. My imagination took over, rendering everything more luscious than it had been. The kiss became longer and longer. We French kissed and explored each other with our tongues. Then she lay down naked on the bed and I covered her flawless body with my kisses the way men did in the novels I had read. Somewhere in the course of the fantasy, I shot my load into my pajamas and had to change. I didn't care. It was the first night I was at peace with my dick, since god knows when.

By the morning it was all over. While I continued to fantasise about Maya for weeks, any chance of meeting her again was gone. My parents and brother had nixed her sister unanimously. My mother thought she was far too outspoken to be a good daughter-in-law. My father had reservations about her parents; according to him, the man was cowed down by the woman who was far too controlling and probing. Both of them had an issue with Maya wearing lipstick at the tender age of sixteen. This just isn't the family for us, they agreed. Bhaiya didn't say much, beyond concurring with them.

Almost twenty-five years passed before I met Maya again, at a party in Gurgaon. She was married to a corporate big-shot and looked stunning in a black off-shoulder dress. Her eyes were as beautiful as ever, and her breasts, every bit as promising under the dress. When I reminded her about us, she broke into peals of laughter. 'This time I'm not just laughing at you,' she said. 'I am laughing at both of us.'

'One day I'll write a story about us,' I told her.

Her eyes narrowed. For an instant, I saw the face from the past telling me to keep my mouth shut or else. 'Make sure you change all the names,' she said in a curt voice, 'and don't ever mention—'

The House Help

TABISH KHAIR

WHEN LOKESH WOKE up, his first feeling was relief at finding that his wife was not sleeping next to him. She had woken up earlier; he could hear her clattering about in the kitchen of their three-bedroom flat. He lay there quietly. The early summer sun beat against the curtains. There was very little traffic noise. It was Sunday. Lokesh was a man of habits; he had ingrained many of his habits into his wife too. One of his habits, which she had adopted, was weekly sex: every Sunday morning to be exact. And Lokesh would always oblige. The process was fixed: they would wake up, the maid would bring them tea in bed, and then, stand there, waiting for her shopping orders. This was part of the process. The maid was sent out, every Sunday morning, to buy breakfast from a particular mithai-wallah in the next colony. She was given the money for auto fare, and it took her about an hour to get back with jalebis, puris and sundry other purchases. That is the time Lokesh and his wife had to make love. They did not need that long. Lokesh would have an erection by the time the maid left (leaving behind her odour in their bedroom), and usually it would be over in ten minutes. Both Lokesh and his wife would look satisfied – and relieved.

But Lokesh had been dreading this morning. Last Sunday was a fiasco. First, there had been no maid. The previous one

– Rabbo – left all of a sudden, without notice, because of some trouble in her family. This had never happened to Lokesh and his wife before: it was one of the reasons, Lokesh maintained, that he interviewed all the maids. He never left it to his wife. He made sure they were reliable. And they had been, all of them, until Rabbo left without notice about a week ago. On a Friday, just like that; she had walked out on them. So that last Sunday, there had been no maid to take their breakfast order, and things had gone wrong. Lokesh had not been able to get it up. His wife had tried – she had gone so far as to caress it – but it had not helped. Lokesh had closed his eyes and concentrated on images of Padma, which was his usual process. Padma, with her imitation silver trinket dangling on a thread between the cleft of her breasts, preternaturally white against her mahogany skin. Ah Padma, with her strong plump arms, her callused hands. But Padma had refused to appear in his mind.

Lokesh knew why: she had left with the maid. Padma had left with Rabbo.

Lokesh was fourteen or fifteen when he realised that he was not interested in the girls of his class, girls like his cousins, girls who dressed well, smelled good, and looked soft. He was fascinated by Padma. But Lokesh knew nothing about sex – he did not stay in the company of those of his classmates who discussed sex, which in any case, as he rightly intuited, was largely hearsay even for them, and the adults around him pretended that sex did not exist. It was a small town, not this metropolis where Lokesh worked now. Lokesh had been brought up in a particular way by a father who would wade into a crowd to slap a man if he saw him misbehave with a woman he did not even know, and a mother who expected protection from the man in her life; he had been brought up to feel responsible for women. A man was expected to shoulder the burden of the women-folk; women were weak and easy to hurt. Not all the women he knew were like that; his grandmother, for instance, did not strike Lokesh as particularly weak, and her life-long maid, Kurmi, only referred to her own husband, long absent from Kurmi's life, as 'munh-jalla harami', or a 'burnt-face bastard'. But these were old women, whose husbands had died or abandoned them ages ago. Lokesh's aunts and cousins, and his mother, however, he thought, conformed to the pattern of weak women who had to be protected by men.

Padma was an exception to this rule. She had been working for Lokesh's family for a few years; her father was the gardener. But now her breasts had become noticeable to Lokesh, though he pretended not to see them. They were small and firm – melons, the knowing-smirking boys in his class used to call boobs, but, no, Padma did not have melons. Mangoes perhaps, the smaller rounder kind one got early in the summer, Lokesh thought, yes, mangoes – and then he had blushed and forced the image out of his mind.

Padma was around Lokesh's age. She always dressed in salwar kameez that were a bit tight – either because they enabled her to move more freely or in order to save on new clothes – and Lokesh also pretended not to notice that, unlike his female classmates, Padma was neither skinny nor plump. She had rounded legs and soft but perceptible biceps. She was too dark for Lokesh to consider pretty, and she was the daughter of a servant, so he could not really consider her attractive, even if he had known, then, what it really was to be attracted to a woman. Why, apart from that tawdry clasp around her neck, Padma used neither jewellery nor make-up!

❧

That winter vacation Padma would carry Lokesh's kid brother around and they played elaborate games in the compound. Lokesh's mother did not worry about them, reposing her faith more in Padma than in Lokesh, so long as they returned to the house on hearing the honking of Papa's car at the gate.

Lokesh remembers that day with surprising clarity. He had been flying a kite on the rooftop of their old ancestral mansion. Padma had come along to mind Lokesh's kid brother; if Papa had been home, Lokesh's kid brother would not have been allowed to the roof, even though it had a railing that was higher than the toddler. Papa had rules that provided for guarding against the worst as far as children were concerned, though luckily for Lokesh the rules were relaxed once he was away.

It was a still day and no other kite was up. The sun was strong for a winter afternoon. Once the kite was up, it stayed almost immobile, neither whipped by a breeze nor challenged by other kites. This bored Lokesh's kid brother. He spent an hour chasing the striped squirrels that clambered up and down the house. They were not particularly timid and would allow you to get to within a foot of them before scampering away. Then he grew sleepy, climbed on to Padma's lap and fell asleep. It was time for his afternoon nap. Lokesh wound up the kite. Padma carried the toddler down to the second floor – there were, as on the ground floor, four self-contained bedroom 'units', which were hardly used.

Padma put him to bed in one of the vacant rooms. These 'guest-rooms' were almost bare, apart from a bed or two in each, sometimes a half-broken chair. There was lots of space to tumble around. Lokesh does not recall how it happened, but suddenly he and Padma were wrestling playfully in the room. There was something exciting about it; he did not feel it was wrong but he also knew they would not have done it in the compound or downstairs, where they could be discovered by others. But almost no one came up to the second floor, except, once a week, when Lokesh's mother led a maid or two up to dust the section, change the bedcovers, and wash the floors.

Lokesh thinks it started with an arm wrestle, which he won with some effort; he was at least a foot taller, and bigger. While Lokesh was not the sportiest of boys in class, he was bigger than most boys and reasonably strong; once or twice when he had been bullied in school, Lokesh had been able to defend himself successfully. As such, he was surprised that when the arm wrestle turned into a full-fledged wrestle, he could not get Padma down. They were wrestling silently. They grappled for twenty minutes, in careful silence, barefoot, until sensing Lokesh losing stamina, Padma wrapped a sinewy leg around his knee and brought him down. There was a soft whump. They disengaged, to listen for an enquiry from downstairs. Nothing was forthcoming.

'I beat you,' Padma whispered to Lokesh.

'I had stopped,' Lokesh argued, and added, 'Anyway, I would have gotten out.'

'No, you wouldn't. No boy ever gets out from under me, if I manage to bring him down,' she boasted.

'How many boys have you wrestled?'

'More than you can imagine,' she replied. Then she added, 'And bigger, stronger boys than you.'

Lokesh had never been truly excited by a girl before. Now he was. His throat felt parched. Had he realised that it was 'sex', a word that he knew only as three alphabets and never heard uttered by adults around him, Lokesh would have disentangled and withdrawn. He knew that sex meant being responsible for the woman involved, even though he had no clear idea what it involved. Even the hip-thrusting in Bombay film songs, which had started by then, held a totally innocent connotation for Lokesh. But this was play, Lokesh half-believed and half-pretended; this much he could allow himself, despite the hard-on that he had.

'You want me to prove it, *boy*?' Padma asked with a smile, challenging and afraid at the same time. It was the first time she had addressed Lokesh with such a familiar term, 'boy.' She knew she was taking a liberty. It was strangely exciting.

Lokesh nodded. He did not feel he could speak normally.

'Lie down on your back,' she instructed.

Lokesh lay down. She climbed on top of him, spread-eagling his arms and legs, and said, 'Now try to throw me off, *boy*.'

He tried. He almost did. She pushed his arms apart and intertwined her legs around his legs, and pushed Lokesh flat on his back again. Her necklace drooped on his face. She laughed and shook her head slowly, tickling him with the silvery clasp at the end of her necklace. He pushed her back, gripping her shoulders, savouring the ripple of soft muscles under her tight kameez. He tried to shove her back by pushing against her stomach, which was surprisingly flat and hard – flatter and harder than Lokesh's. After minutes of soundless struggle,

Lokesh gave up. He was breathing hard, sweat beads trickling down his sideburns.

'See, I am not even out of breath,' Padma whispered. She did not get off him. She put her head down on his shoulder and lay like that. She had a strong, musty smell, quite unlike the smell of any woman or of any girl from Lokesh's class. It aroused him even further. Lokesh could feel the hardness in his pants. She could feel it too. The world was quiet; Lokesh had never felt as much at peace with the world. (Much later, he learned to recognise that moment of oneness with the world in the seconds – the soundless seconds that always broke too soon – between coming and beginning to turn away.)

They just lay there for minutes, breathing against one another, maybe ten, maybe even twenty minutes, until Lokesh's kid brother showed signs of waking up. Then they jumped apart and pretended nothing had happened.

That was eighteen years ago. Now, lying in his fancy metropolitan flat, with his wife – educated, perfumed, soft – pottering about in their stylish kitchen, Lokesh could hardly recall Padma's features. He remembered her smell though. But it was the first time in eighteen years that he was unable to recall Padma's features, thought Lokesh. She had left two years later, during which they had often wrestled together. They had never made love though. Lokesh would get up after a wrestling bout, which Padma always won (Lokesh did not wish it otherwise), go into a bathroom and jerk off. But he never made love to Padma. Despite the one occasion – his parents had been away – on which she tugged at his pyjama-string and pulled down his pyjamas. That had frightened Lokesh. He had pulled together his pyjamas and rushed away. After that, Lokesh thinks, he avoided Padma, and soon she left – to be married off, his parents told him.

Lokesh lay in his bed – relieved that his wife had not expected sex from him this morning – and realised with a shock that he had long forgotten Padma's features. It was not just this morning. He had years ago mixed up Padma's features with other faces. Had he imagined the necklace too? No, that he remembered, its imitation silver clasp brushing his face, hanging lightly even as Padma pinned him down, surprisingly heavy for her size. But the rest of Padma? When he thought back, he recalled a sequence of Padmas – with the features of the maids he had hired. They had looked different from Padma at times, he was sure, but they had all been sturdily built young women, used to carrying weights and doing chores. Women who wore no jewellery that was worth anything. Women who looked and smelled very different from his cousins, classmates, female colleagues, and his lovely, sophisticated wife, who had a safe deposit box for her jewellery in their bank. They had left a similar sweat-hair oil-and-talcum body smell in the bedroom every Sunday morning. Padma had arisen in Lokesh's mind, Sunday after Sunday, out of the miasma of that ghostly smell.

'We have to find a new house help soon,' he shouted to his wife. 'We cannot have you wasting your Sunday mornings making breakfast for us.' Then he lay back and wondered whether it was still too early in the summer to get mangoes from the vendors outside.

Chunni Lal

ADITYA SHARMA

I DON'T KNOW why my parents named me Chunni Lal when there were hundreds of better names to pick from. While it made me the butt of jokes, it wasn't my name that troubled me. What did was something I couldn't talk about openly. But my close friends knew about it: my out-of-control libido. They used to call me 'tharki' – a nickname I hated. I found it unfair and judgmental. Is it my fault that God has made me a little different and I feel all the time this desperate urge to screw every girl I see?

But girls are a slippery lot. Unless, of course, you are blessed with the four virtues of money, overconfidence, cunning, and a way with words. I am not. I am, however, tall, fair, and reasonably handsome. But that was no help. My success rate with women was dismal.

It was after my matriculation that my quest for sex acquired an extra urgency. I propositioned girls I saw on the road, in the park, on trains and buses, in hospitals, and once in a zoo. But having no idea how to approach them, I flopped time and again.

My first big opportunity to open my account came when I was in class eleven. It didn't happen all of a sudden. I had known Megha from childhood. We had grown up playing and studying together. Senior to me by a year, she was a class twelve student at Devgarh's Jain Girls High School. She lived opposite my house across the street. A class topper, she helped with my lessons, and what's more, wore a skirt. Her family thought me a decent kid. But when no one was around, I would put my hand on her thigh but she would push it away.

Adding fuel to my fire was Megha's older brother, Mayur. He was my sole supplier of porn magazines. Back in the 1990s there were no smart phones, and computers were not common. All you had were magazines like *Debonair* and *Fantasy*. If you had to watch a porn film, you needed to get a VCR or a VCP along with a Double X (mild sex) or a Triple X (hardcore sex) video cassette, depending on your taste. Mayur, too, was sex-obsessed like me but a duffer in studies. Envious of my good marks, he wanted to take my mind off studies by getting me hooked to porn. Little did he realise that what he was preaching would one day be practised on his own sister.

Megha was taller than her friends. For her age, she had a big ass and the curves of an adult. She had big black eyes, a round face, and a broad forehead. One day I went to her house to seek her help with a difficult problem in physics. It was the middle of summer. Three in the afternoon. Her folks were asleep. Megha sat on a chair reading, her feet up on a stool. My eyes went straight to her milky thighs – and what do I see next! She wasn't wearing a panty. I gasped. This was my life's first glimpse of cunt. It was like Nature had folded a pair of lips vertically between her legs. I slipped my left hand beneath her skirt and my right under her shoulder. Before she could realise what was going on I'd lifted her off the chair. 'Leave me, I say. Somebody might come!' she whispered fiercely.

'Why don't you jump down?' I said, teasing. My organ was stiff as a metal pipe. As I held her, my left hand crawled further into her skirt.

'Leave me!' She tried to wriggle free but couldn't.

Afraid that somebody from her family might walk in, I set her down. She glared at me, outraged, but also thrilled. She neither admonished me, nor said anything to encourage me. She settled down again in her chair with a book in hand as if nothing had happened.

Though I had an all-consuming sex drive, I retained enough sense to know I couldn't afford to neglect my studies. After my father died, my mother and older brother opened a small grocery shop near our house. There was never enough money. I knew that the only way out of our genteel poverty was for me to become an engineer and get a well-paying job.

Two weeks later, when I went to Megha's house, I saw her writing furiously in her notebook. She was stretched out on the divan in the living room, a white shawl over her legs. Without looking up, she asked me to come back later as her parents and brother were out, gone to attend a wedding. I couldn't believe my luck. Megha was all alone in the house!

Ignoring her directive to leave, I sat down next to her. 'You are always studying! Don't you ever get bored?'

'Bored? I have chemistry class test tomorrow.' Then she caught me looking at her. 'Go back to your house, Chunni.'

I put a hand on her legs. She swatted it away. I thrust my hand into her shawl.

'Stop it,' she ordered.

'I just want to touch you, that's all! Are you afraid of me?'

'Afraid of you? No way!'

I pushed my hand inside her skirt and let it rest on her knickers. Unable to control me – or herself – she seemed so vulnerable.

'You have several panties: red, blue, green...' I said, slowly tracing the vertical line of her cunt.

'How do you know?'

'I often catch a glimpse, chori-chori.'

She smiled. I bent over her and kissed her lips. I kissed her a second time and drew back. Her face had turned red as a beetroot. I threw the shawl off her legs and kissed her thighs. When I tried to pull down her skirt, she grabbed my hands.

'Wait a minute,' she said. Getting off the divan, Megha went to the door and bolted it from inside.

Coming back, she lay down again, pretending to read her chemistry book.

I snatched the book, put it on the stool and slid my right hand into her bra. What a delicious shock it was, to fondle a girl's breasts for the first time in my life! I had no idea they would be this soft. Megha held on to my hands when I tried to take off her bra. 'Somebody might come,' she pleaded.

But she didn't protest when I pulled down her skirt and panty. It was apparent she wanted to fuck, but she would have me remove only what needed to be dislodged for the purpose.

I had reckoned that the point of entry would be somewhere north of her pussy. But despite probing it with my fingers for close to five minutes, I failed to locate it. What the hell. Suddenly an idea crossed my mind. If I just lay on her, my penis was bound to find the 'hole' wherever it was. So I began rubbing my organ up and down her cunt. For a moment it felt like my penis was on to something but I wasn't sure if it had found its mark. Wherever it was, it felt heavenly. I wanted the bliss to last awhile but unable to hold myself, ejaculated.

Disentangling myself from Megha, as I sat on the bed, I could see my white discharge gleaming on her pubic hair. She put on her skirt and said, 'I must wash myself.' Taking her panty along, she headed straight to the bathroom.

When she came back, she said, 'Do you even know how to do it?' The contempt in her voice hurt. Flopping in my first attempt was a massive blow to my ego but I hoped Megha would give me another chance.

I never found her alone again. On a couple of occasions when my mother and brothers had gone out, I urged her to come over but she refused. On the days I visited her, I found her wearing slacks beneath the skirt so I couldn't feel her thighs. It was obvious she was put off by my incompetence.

A few weeks later, on Rakshabandhan, I was chatting with Megha's cousins at her home. After she had tied the rakhi thread on their hands, one of them suggested she should tie a rakhi on my hand too. He thought since I didn't have a sister, having one would make me happy.

'I don't believe in these rituals,' I said quickly.

But Megha walked up and stood before me, expecting me to give her my hand. I stepped back in horror. 'You want to avoid giving me money, is it?' she taunted.

I was shocked. Was this attempt to make me her rakhi brother a ploy to ensure I stayed away from her? I stared at her, disbelieving, then turned around and hurried to the door. As I stepped out, my parting shot to her was, 'Yes, I want to save money.'

After that day I stopped going to Megha's house. Even when

our paths crossed in the street I didn't feel like talking to her. A
year later, when I got admission in a regional engineering college,
I left Devgarh. Around the time of my graduation Megha got
married and moved to her husband's home in Delhi. Recently,
my mother happened to meet her. She told me Megha is now
twice her former size and a mother of two.

Once it tastes human blood, the tiger, people say, becomes a
man-eater. Having tasted a girl, it was natural I would begin
hunting for my next prey. God knows I was hungry. But Devgarh
afforded few opportunities.

I began to accost women almost at random. But I was
so tactless and overeager that even the unloveliest wouldn't
agree. Sometimes I followed them home. I was warned but
I persisted. One day I was thrashed by the girl's brother. We
happened to be right in front of her house when I grabbed
her hand and he had seen me.

I had been following her for days. It was her smile that had
emboldened me to try something romantic, and so I had. A few
neighbours suggested I should be handed over to the police. But
thankfully, when the outraged brother saw blood oozing from
my nose he let me go. I stopped following women thereafter.
The only outlet for my frustration was masturbation. I jerked
off three, sometimes four, times a day.

My next opportunity came four years later, in the final year of
my engineering degree. I came home for Diwali and found a
beautiful guest. Sharda was my bhabhi's eighteen-year-old sister.

It did strike me as not a very decent thing to do – to lust after your own relative. But I decided it was less dangerous than trying my luck with strangers on the street.

With thick lips, a shapely nose, and a high forehead, Sharda exuded a sweet sensuousness. Her breasts and bottom were oversized for her petite figure. Her complexion was on the darker side. She had one of those physiques where the flesh is evenly distributed across the frame and it gave me a hard-on every time she passed by, her hips swinging pendulum-like with every step. Once I saw her get up from a chair. Her kurti clung to the fold of her buttocks. For a moment she seemed bare-bottomed. My head spun in maddening desire. But with so many people around, it was easy to fantasise but difficult to execute.

My brother and his new wife had their own room. Sharda slept in my mother's room. There were two more cots in the room I shared with my younger brother, who had lost about eighty percent of his vision after a severe bout of chickenpox in his early childhood.

Before long I came up with an idea. My mother always wakes up early to bathe, pray and prepare breakfast for all of us. If I got up just when she leaves the room, I could try my luck with Sharda without anyone noticing. There was the danger that she could raise an alarm. But no risk meant no returns. I also felt encouraged by the fact that Sharda had smiled at me the night before. As they say, hansi to fansi! My mind was taken over by images of Sharda naked in my arms, tantalising me through the night. Despite jerking off thrice my hunger showed no sign of abating. At about five, when I heard the tinkling of my mother's bracelets, I knew the golden hour had arrived. As I heard my mother close the door from outside, I threw off my blanket.

Sharda was fast asleep. I checked on Aashu, my younger brother. His gentle snores were reassuring. My heart thumping, I sat down beside Sharda. She didn't stir. I kissed her hand. Nothing. I kissed her face. She turned a little. But when I kissed her lips, she woke up with a start and sat on the cot, staring at me in shock. 'Mother is gone,' I whispered to her, to assure her that nobody was watching. 'And Aashu is sleeping. Even if he wakes up, he won't be able to see anything.'

She held my hand as I pushed it inside her blanket. I caught her by the shoulders and tried to kiss her but an outraged Sharda shoved me back with such force it was obvious she was angry. Undeterred, I slipped my hand under her blanket and caressed her thighs. I sat expecting another rebuff, maybe a slap, but to my surprise, she did nothing. Emboldened, I began working my fingers in a circular motion around her cunt. Before she could push me away again, I slid under her warm blanket, caught her by the waist and began kissing her neck and face. I squeezed her bottom and slowly traced their wide curve with my fingers. I think Sharda was sufficiently aroused by then. When I tried to undo the knot of her salwar, she didn't stop me. 'What if someone comes?' she whispered.

I got up, bolted the door from inside. After pulling her salwar down, I went for her panty, and found that she wasn't wearing one. Moving from the soft warm skin of her thighs, my hand toyed with the coils of her pubic hair.

I began fondling her breasts. But like Megha, she wouldn't let me remove her bra.

'Somebody might come, please leave,' she whispered in mock anger.

Without wasting any more time, I got into position on

top of her. But once again, I didn't know where exactly to put it. My fingers failed to find the opening. I tried pushing into her from different angles, desperate to succeed this time. My hands clutching her breasts, I tried penetrating her for close to five minutes. But once again, I failed to find the opening, and ejaculated.

Sharda saw the discharge on her and said, 'I need to get rid of this.' As I was giving her my underwear to clean herself, there was a knock on the door. 'Sharda, O Sharda, why have you locked the door from inside?' It was her sister! Goodness, how had she woken up so early! I motioned Sharda to open the door and rushed to my bed. It took her a while to scrub my cum off her body, tie her salwar, and open the door. But in her confusion, she forgot to hide my underwear. When her sister entered the room she couldn't help but notice my VIP trunks lying under Sharda's cot.

Soon, Bhabhi extracted the entire truth from her sister. Later that morning, my furious sister-in-law charged me with sullying her family's honour. 'You could do this because we are poor,' she screamed. I had no choice but to listen to her lecture. All the while my older brother kept up a serious face but my younger one could barely control his laughter. Thankfully my mother didn't make a fuss about it. 'You shouldn't have done this, Chunni,' she said to me in front of everyone, making it obvious to my bhabhi that I had been properly ticked off and she need not rant and rave any further.

Sharda was packed off to her home the same evening and I never saw her again.

I finished my engineering at twenty-two, and got my first job in the neighbouring industrial town of Sherpur. After Sharda, I met a couple of girls whom I could have bedded, but failed for one reason or another. Two girls whom I managed to befriend ditched me after making me poorer by a few thousand rupees in different restaurants. One girl I charmed into coming to my room would only let me kiss her. She vanished after extracting from me a branded jeans and an expensive silk top. Then there was this woman who lived alone in my locality. On hearing that her husband worked in a different city, I went to her home and asked if we could be of some use to each other. At first she didn't understand. When I made my intentions explicit, she yelled, 'Get out of my house, you rascal!'

I was twenty-seven when my mother asked me to attend her guruji's satsang in Lohana, a town not far from my factory. Since it was a Saturday, and I had an afternoon shift on Monday, I decided to go. Even my roommate was visiting his family for the weekend and I didn't want to be on my own.

Mother had been attending guruji's satsangs for years but I found them boring. Guruji repeated the same old homilies: Life is short, we all have to die one day, we must be kind to others, work hard, do this, do that….

A satsang could, however, be an interesting place if you're looking to meet girls. And that's what happened. During the tea break, when I went to see my mother in the women's section, I saw her talking to a girl who was about my age. Average height, wheatish complexion, she was plain-looking. But her erect, rounded breasts were eye-grabbing. A tad too large for her build, they seemed to be looking for someone to liberate them from her blue kurta. She wore a contrasting white pathani salwar and her hair fell on her shoulders in luxuriant profusion. 'Here he comes,' my mother said to the girl. From the way she looked at me, I could make out mother had been talking about me.

'Shall I get you some tea?' I asked my mother. 'The sevadaars (volunteers) are serving tea and snacks over there,' I said, nodding at the shamiana nearby.

'Get us four cups, I have three more friends here.'

I wanted to hug her and say thank you when she pointed at the girl and said, 'Take Nidhi along, the two of you can hold two cups each.'

As we stood in a queue of devotees waiting for free tea and snacks, Nidhi said, 'You are an engineer?'

I nodded.

'Your mother is worried about your marriage.'

'That's her favourite worry,' I said, feigning disinterest.

'What kind of girl do you like?'

'Me? Someone simple, loving...' I fumbled for the right words. Despite the question, I could sense that it was Nidhi who was actually assessing me as marriage material.

'My father too has been scouting boys for me. But most of them demand dowry, which he can ill-afford.'

'Is he also here at the satsang?' I asked, anxious that he might be eying us now.

'I've come with a friend. She's sitting with your mother.'

After the tea break, the satsang resumed, and the loudspeakers resonated with guruji's raspy voice. I kept looking at Nidhi. But her eyes were fixed on guruji. She didn't glance at me once.

It was a two-day satsang and I met Nidhi again the next

morning over tea. In her pink sari and low-cut, matching blouse, she looked striking. No matter how hard I tried, I couldn't help staring at her cleavage. 'Come, let's sit here,' I said. 'We can talk in some privacy.'

She mutely walked with me to the garden adjacent to the discourse complex. There was nobody around and as we stood facing each other, I took her hand in mine and lied, 'You know, I've studied palmistry.'

Her eyes opened wide, and she held out her hand. 'Tell me something then.'

Tracing a line on her palm, I said, 'Your fate line is prominent. This means you'll have a very comfortable life. I can also see that you'll get married soon.'

Her eyes glowed with excitement when she heard that.

Instead of telling her more, I pulled her towards me and tried to hug her. She pushed me away.

'Will you marry me?' she asked, pointblank.

Nidhi's father had retired years ago. To support her family she worked as a primary school teacher, drawing a measly five thousand rupees a month. I knew my mother wouldn't accept a girl who could not bring sufficient dowry.

'I hardly know you,' I said, 'How can I say I'll marry you?'

She fell quiet. I made bold to ask her, 'Why don't you come to my place in Sherpur? It's just twenty kilometres from here. We can chat about this in peace and get to know each other better.'

She mulled over the proposition. To my utter surprise she agreed. 'I'll inform my friend that I'm visiting a relative and skipping the rest of the discourse. Wait for me here.'

Soon I was sitting beside my 'young catch' in the Sherpur-bound state transport bus, my dick hard as a gear stick. I held

Nidhi's hand in mine. Every time the bus lurched, I pressed my thigh against hers, picturing in my head how she'd look minus the sari.

'Select or reject?' she said, shaking me out of my fantasy.

'What do you mean?'

'It means,' she explained coyly, 'do you consider me good enough to marry?'

'How can I say that now?' I said. 'Let's reach my place. We'll know soon enough if we are meant for each other.'

By now other passengers were staring at us. It was obvious to them we were not married, and the sight of a young romantic couple travelling together in a bus was a rarity in these parts. As the bus conductor eyed us suspiciously, I disengaged our thighs and handed him the fare.

The walk from the bus stand to my room was not an easy one. With Nidhi by my side, I had to brave the leering shopkeepers and knowing looks from the neighbours who knew me. To compound my discomfort, my dick wouldn't relent. I had to hold my handbag in front to hide the prominent bulge from view.

Fortunately for me, the landlord wasn't home. I unlocked my room and ushered Nidhi in. She sat down on the bed – there were no chairs – mopping the sweat off her brow. I switched on the fan and sat next to her. I wanted to talk to her to break the uneasy silence but my throat was dry. I was so drenched in lust that my dick throbbed painfully in the confines of my trunks. I wondered if Nidhi had seen it poking against my trousers.

I had a makeshift kitchen in the room. Nidhi saw the utensils and stove and offered to make tea. 'Do you have some milk?'

To my surprise, there was. My miserly roommate had left some that morning before leaving for work. In no time Nidhi was boiling tea leaves in our blackened pan. I couldn't control myself any longer. I hugged her from behind, cupping her breasts, my dick prodding the crevice of her buttocks. 'Leave me,' she said, 'Do you want me to scald myself over the stove?'

We sat down on the bed, sipping hot tea. The moment she placed her empty cup on the table I grabbed her again. I pushed her down on the bed, thrust my hand into her sari and began kneading her thighs. Nidhi let my hand move freely. But when I reached for her panty, she clasped my hand.

I saw her studying me intently. I held her face in my hands and planted a gentle kiss on her cheek.

'With what right did you kiss me?' Her expression and her tone, half-serious, half-coy.

It was apparent she wanted to hear me say that I love her or something romantic but I didn't want to raise her expectations. 'Because you are my friend,' I mumbled. I pulled her towards me and tried to hug her again but the bed creaked dolefully, as if warning me to leave the girl.

'Shall we shift to the mattress on the floor?' I suggested.

Nidhi gave me a knowing smile. 'What do you plan to do there?'

Burning with lust, I picked her up and set her down on my roommate's mattress. Then I lay on top of her, covering her lips with hungry kisses.

She drew back to ask, 'Will you marry me?' Ignoring her question, I got her sari out of the way. Her belly was smooth and flat. I moved my lips on its soft warm skin. I put my hands on her ultra-tight blouse and gently squeezed her breasts. She moaned, her eyes half-closed. I made her turn around, and as she lay facing the floor, I removed her blouse. I peeled off her petticoat, exposing the soft orbs of her bottom converging like two muskmelons placed side by side. Unhooking her bra, I made her turn again and found myself facing her kind and wonderful breasts. A few gentle squeezes made the pink nipples expand like the petals of a flower.

I took off my shirt and vest. As my skin came in contact with hers, an electric current passed through my body. Or so it felt. I sucked her nipples. She moaned. I clasped her panty and tried to pull it down. But it was knotted so tightly it refused to move. I took off my pants. She saw my erect organ protruding through the underwear and asked, 'Will you marry me?'

'Yes,' I said. 'Help me remove your panty.'

'Do you mean it?' Her hand went down and her panty came magically unstuck. All it needed was a gentle pull to bring down the final barrier. But the serious tone in which she spoke made me pause. What if after sex, she becomes adamant that I marry her? Then I panicked. What if she files a police complaint accusing me of having sex with her on a false promise of marriage? I could end up in jail. I had heard of women misusing the law to marry somebody forcibly or extort a hefty sum to drop the charge. I wasn't going to be the next victim.

Painful as it was, I curbed myself. I did not remove my underwear or her panty. I just lay on top of her. If you can't have sex with a girl, nobody can stop you from imagining that you are having sex with her. Separated by two slim layers of undergarments, I moved my dick over her cunt, back and forth, back and forth, imagining I was fucking her.

'What's this?' asked Nidhi, disappointed, 'Do it properly.'

Do it properly, is it? I smiled to myself. And go to jail? Nidhi rani, don't consider me a fool. Women like you not only want to have fun but also trap men into marriage.

Soon enough, I came in my underwear. I got up, leaving her dissatisfied. She was glaring at me. I got out of my soiled underwear and slipped into my pants, leaving a panty-clad Nidhi on the mattress. Embarrassed, she too began to dress, asking me not to look.

Combing her hair before our broken mirror, she wanted to know, 'What have you decided about marriage?'

'You talk as if it's my decision alone. I have a mother and she also has to approve of you. And our horoscopes have to match.'

'Are you saying you won't marry me? Did you bring me here to satisfy your lust?'

I knew I had to pacify her. 'Look, Nidhi, I like you a lot. But how can I marry without my mother's approval? As for bringing you here, didn't I control myself in time? Tell me?'

'Mazze le gaye, and now you are mouthing this nonsense. Why didn't you take your dear mother's approval before tricking me into your room?'

I wanted to tell her that she too had enjoyed herself. How she was moaning in pleasure a short while ago. But I didn't want to stoke her rage. So I humoured her. 'Once we know that our horoscopes match, my mother would certainly agree. After all, she also wants me to get married.'

When I suggested I could drop her to the bus stand, Nidhi showed no sign of getting up from the bed. Instead she burst out, 'I have given you the most important thing any girl can give to a man. Nobody has dared to touch me like that before.'

Clearly, she was in no mood to leave without extracting a promise of marriage. I looked at the clock: I had about an hour to report to the factory. 'The landlord might come here any moment and create a scene,' I said, 'let's get going.'

She got up instantly. Perhaps she'd had a nasty experience with a landlord before. As I walked with her to the bus stand, suffering those leery looks all over again, I almost convinced her that I'd try my best to marry her. But I knew she didn't stand a chance.

'Don't worry,' I said, passing the ticket to her through the bus window. 'God willing, we shall meet soon.'

Seeing Nidhi off took such a toll on my mind that I was taken aback to discover that my feet were carrying me not to the factory but in the opposite direction. I stopped, assured myself that a catastrophe had been averted, and took an auto-rickshaw to reach the factory just on time.

Two days later, I received Nidhi's horoscope. Several calls on my mobile followed. Each time the same question: 'When are we marrying?' Exasperated, I told her that our horoscopes had sarpdosh, a fatal defect. 'Our panditji has warned that if we marry, one of us will die.' That made her quiet for a while. But she called back within an hour to say she wanted to meet the panditji. 'You would have to ask my mother,' I said. 'I've no idea where he lives.'

By then I had cribbed to my mother about how Nidhi was pestering me to marry her. I didn't forget to add that she couldn't afford a decent dowry but omitted to mention the incident in my room. So when Nidhi called her, my mother spoke to her so harshly she didn't call me after that. I thanked my stars for having given me the good sense to stop in the nick of time.

Had the 'act' been committed, I doubt if Nidhi would have spared me.

❧

The Nidhi episode left me so scarred that I agreed to marry a Jaipur-based girl suggested by a relative even though she was no beauty. But she looked homely and good-natured. Her father was a government servant and had a big bungalow. My mother assumed she would bring a good dowry. I wasn't bothered about the money though. I was marrying for sex. I just wanted the girl to be a virgin like me. It was impossible to ask about this directly. So when we first met I made a silly generalisation, 'These days women get intimate with men even before their marriage.'

She looked at me as if I'd insulted her. 'Mister, do I look like a loose woman to you?'

'Come on, Anu, I wasn't referring to you,' I said, dropping the matter then and there. From her hurt tone and expression, I concluded she was speaking the truth.

It's a complicated business, getting married. Holding on to the hope of finally being able to fuck, I managed to survive the countless boring rituals. When it was all over and I brought Anu home in a car, it seemed like I'd won a trophy in a sports championship.

'You must be an expert by now,' joked a married older cousin as I headed for the room where my bride awaited me. It was our suhaag raat. I would have asked him for some tips but I didn't want to advertise my ignorance.

I had watched two porn films the previous week and was surprised by how easy it all seemed. But even after a close study

of the various positions enacted in the films, I had little clarity
on the exact location of the opening and the appropriate angle
of entry. I was not sure how much the exciting theory lessons
would help me in practice.

Anu smiled at me as she saw me bolt the door from inside.
She was fair, and a little too slim for my taste. I would have
preferred more curves. She had small, pert breasts and a modest
posterior. What I liked most about her was her smile. It exposed
her bright uneven teeth which lit up her otherwise ordinary
face. Her thick long hair in a tight braid, her angular body
gift-wrapped in a beautiful sari, and with all her jewellery and
make-up and heavenly perfume, I found her irresistible.

I sat down on the bed beside her, happy in the knowledge
that my lifelong ambition to enter a woman was about to be
fulfilled. I spent a few minutes making small talk about the
wedding function, and about the relatives who'd attended. Then I
pulled her towards me and kissed her on the mouth, swallowing
her scented lipstick in the process. I began to caress her smooth
belly and gently pushed her down on the bed. I put my arms
around her and drew her closer to me. Feeling up her bottom I
was disappointed to find not enough flesh down there. Kissing
her face, neck and shoulders, I said, 'Why don't you change
into something simple like a salwar or a gown? You have on so
much jewellery, it's obstructing…'

'Obstructing what?' she said, smiling.

I was pleased that unlike Megha and Sharda, my wife was
not shy about sex. Without much ado she got up from the bed.
'Give me a minute.'

'You can change right here,' I said, 'I won't look at you, I
promise.'

But she went to the door behind the almirah to undress. And then, I remembered something that made me jump. The foolish woman didn't know there was a big crack in the door facing the street and it was likely that one of my prurient neighbours was looking through it right now. I rushed to her and caught her completely in the buff. She was about to admonish me, but seeing my face, realised something was wrong. When I pointed to the thumb-sized rupture in the door, she ran back to the bed, leaving her clothes on the floor.

'Get my gown from the almirah!' Her voice was so loud I was sure everyone in the house had heard. Imagine a newly-wed wife commanding her husband to fetch her gown on her very first night! What would my brothers, Bhabhi and mother think?

I was on the verge of saying something sharp. But when I saw her sitting on the bed stark naked, my anger was swiftly replaced by lust. Switching off the light, I got rid of my wedding suit and jumped on the bed clad only in my underwear. Another round of frenetic kissing followed. I pressed and squeezed and kneaded her breasts till she moaned in pleasure. Then I took her nipples in my mouth. I turned her over and kissed her back. Her skin was so soft it felt divine to just lie on her, absorbing her body heat and feminine smell. I pulled down my underwear and His Hardness rammed straight into her ass.

'Not there,' she groaned. 'It's hurting.'

I rolled her 180 degrees. It was dark except for some faint light coming through the cracked glass of the window. I could make out the outline of her face and resumed kissing and licking her lips. I felt my pubic hair rub against hers and my dick lodged itself in the vicinity of her cunt. Using my knees to raise myself, I guided my little brother to his destination.

Or tried to. I tried every possible angle known to man. But the damn hole eluded me yet again. Seeing me fumbling for over ten minutes, Anu taunted me, 'You don't even know how to do it?' The words sounded familiar, and I realised I'd heard them before – from Megha.

Feeling slighted, I began thrusting more violently, hoping to somehow get it in the slot. My dick began to hurt a little but I ignored the pain. After a couple of minutes of this, as the pain worsened, I thought I should check my progress. I grabbed my cell phone from the bedside table and held its torch over the conflict zone.

I was excited, and relieved, to see drops of blood around her cunt and on my dick. I had broken her seal! 'Look, your blood!' I said, grinning with joy. Here finally was proof that my wife was a virgin and me a stud. Like a real *mard*, I had deflowered her!

'How could it be?' she exclaimed, peering at the blood under the torchlight.

I smiled, and snapped my fingers, feeling smug.

'Stupid!' she said. 'You were moving your dick in and out of my thighs. It's your blood, not mine!'

I redirected the beam of light at my dick, and realised she was right. A tiny trickle of blood was oozing out of it.

'Get me some Boroline, will you?' I said, horrified. 'Ask Mother, she knows where it's kept.'

'At this hour! What do I tell her?'

'Tell her…uhh…that I've cut my finger?'

'There's a bottle of Dettol near the almirah,' she said. 'Try that instead.'

'Dettol on my dick? Are you crazy?'

It took Anu some time to fetch Boroline from Mother. By then, the blood had clotted but the pain remained. I applied some cream and lay groaning on the bed.

'Sorry for the Dettol suggestion!' Anu said, lying down beside me.

'It's hurting badly,' I muttered. I turned my back on her and fell asleep in no time. It was an unusual suhaag raat, to say the least.

Next morning, I rushed to Dr K.K. Punjabi, our family physician. 'Kya hua?' He was expecting to hear about some common ailment like fever or cold. I wasn't sure how to tell him. Then I figured I had to give him the truth. By the time I finished, the bespectacled doctor whom I had never seen smiling in all these years was laughing uproariously. There was no stopping him. Here was this patient in pain and in need of medical attention and this unfeeling doctor was enjoying himself at his expense!

'Take off your pants,' he barked, still chuckling, 'Let me see the tear.' He inspected my dick with gloved hands. 'I don't think it needs any stitches,' he said. 'But you should abstain from sex for at least ten days. I'll give you some medicines so it heals quickly.'

Ten days! Abstinence! I just got married! How was I to control myself?

Dr Punjabi seemed to know what was going through my mind and smiled impishly. 'Now, remember. Don't put your dick into a woman's thighs. God has created a special place for it. And the next time you go for it, do it slowly. Like this. The crazy doctor stood up and began humping, in slow motion, an imaginary woman in front of him.

Just then Dr Punjabi's nurse walked in. When she saw me standing naked from the waist down and Dr Punjabi performing his bizarre pelvic thrusts, crooning, 'holey-holey, slowly-slowly,' first her mouth fell open, and then her hand went to her mouth. She turned around and fled the room.

'At least knock before entering,' Dr Punjabi yelled after her. Before anyone else could come in and be traumatised by an unexpected sighting of my family jewels, I pulled up my trousers.

'You ruined my image before my own nurse,' Dr Punjabi said, wagging an accusing finger at me. 'God knows what she must think of me now... not that I'm gay, I hope.'

As I paid Dr Punjabi and took the medicines from him, he calmed down. 'Never mind, young man. If you have sex the way I told you, you'll never hurt yourself. But trim that jungle of yours,' he said, pointing to my crotch.

Two days later, Anu and I shifted to my flat in Noida, close to where my new office was located. Even if I couldn't fuck her, there was no stopping me from hugging and kissing her. But every time my dick stiffened, so did the pain. For more than a week I lay torn between desire and self-control. On the ninth day after the tear, as I sat in the office daydreaming about my wife, I realised that the pain had become more bearable. It was finally time to do the deed that's been long overdue.

As soon as the clock struck six, I rushed to my flat, forgetting to even punch my ID card that day. At home I found Anu engrossed in a saas-bahu soap. She was wearing a tight-fitting red top and blue jeans. Now that her mother-in-law was not around, she had switched completely to western outfits. I settled down with her on the sofa and pecked her on the cheek but she barely noticed. Then her serial was interrupted by a commercial break. I took the opportunity to switch off the TV and began squeezing her breasts. Her eyes half-shut, Anu moaned, a little too loudly it seemed to me. It struck me then how differently women moan. While Megha and Nidhi had soft, low-pitched moans, Sharda made an odd, hissing sound. But none of them was as loud as my wife.

I quickly got rid of Anu's jeans and top. As she lay on the sofa in her bra and panty, she could have been one of those models in lingerie advertisements. Kissing her body all over, I unhooked her bra. When I pulled her panty down, I was amused to see that she had shaved off the hair. In my imagination, a woman with a dense bush was wilder and sexier than a clean-shaven one. When I got on top of her, I could feel my pubic hair graze against her hairless crack. Recollecting Dr Punjabi's advice, I began mimicking his pelvic movements, holey-holey.

'What the hell are you doing?' asked an exasperated Anu. 'Chunni, it's all very simple. Just put your dick in the opening and give it a gentle push.'

'But where's the opening?' I said, groping around without a clue.

'Kid, it's not at the top, it's down there.' She took my finger and guided it to the exact spot.

I was astounded to discover that the opening was located – of all places – at the bottom edge of her cunt. I tried sticking my dick in but it kept slipping. After a minute or two of this, Anu again came to my rescue: she grabbed my dick and held it to the opening. 'Until now I hadn't come across anyone who doesn't know how to do it, such a simple thing!' she said, her voice rising in irritation. 'Now push it inside.'

I did as I was told. Ah, how smoothly my dick slid in! It was exquisite to have my manhood engulfed in the tight warmth of her cunt. I was so electrified by my first experience of cunt that I squirted almost instantaneously.

Even before I could pull out, Anu made her disappointment obvious. 'You have a big dick but so little patience.'

We fucked three more times that night. I still had trouble finding the slot but Anu bailed me out each time. Once we did it with her on top and she did a far better job of riding me than I had of her. It was her idea to also try the doggie style.

'How do you know all these positions?' I asked her, astonished.

'I… well, I learnt about them from a book.'

Thank goodness that unlike me, my wife at least knew a few things about sex. Without her support, I would have failed yet again. A huge weight off my shoulders, I slept like a baby that night.

The next day I took Anu out for dinner to a Chinese restaurant. Later we went to a nearby park for ice-cream. On a bench a few metres from where we sat was a young couple, smooching away to glory with scant regard for anyone else around. 'What shameless people!' I said, disgusted.

'What's so shameless about it?' said Anu. 'Everyone has an affair or two in college. Didn't you have a girlfriend?'

'Not me,' I said, 'Did you have an affair?'

My wife looked at me hesitantly, as if debating the right answer. 'Well…no, but most of my friends did.'

Instead of enjoying the ice-cream, I found myself trying to join the dots, connecting Anu's words and her performance last night. She had found my dick quite big. Didn't that mean she had seen a smaller dick – or several small dicks? I also remembered that she'd said, 'Until now I hadn't come across anyone who doesn't know how to do it'. So how many expert lovers had she had until now? And her reaction to this couple kissing in full public view was so casual. Only someone who had 'been there, done it all' could possibly consider their behaviour normal. It was becoming obvious to me that Anu wasn't the virgin I had assumed her to be. Only an experienced veteran could have taught me three different ways to fuck in our very first encounter.

I had waited years to experience the bliss of carnal union. The quest was finally over. While I've tasted mostly failure in the sport of lovemaking, my wife has turned out to be a champion of sorts. Not in my wildest dreams of sex did I imagine that in addition to the bliss, it would also leave me with a broken heart and an inferiority complex.

The Real Sex

AMRITA CHATTERJEE

IT HAPPENED VERY quietly, like witnessing a robbery on a deserted highway. At dusk, on a balmy April night, I found myself in Pune, waiting to see a man who had made me an offer I couldn't refuse. We had met a few days ago, in the dark, as lovers always do. He looked at me sideways while swirling the ice cubes in a whiskey glass with his big, fleshy hands. Then he smiled. I'd already had a bit too much to drink, so I smiled back.

'I like your hands,' I said. It was meant to be a compliment but it came out as a request.

'Do you? Well... merci.' He bowed his head like a shy schoolboy.

'Would you like to dance?'

'Me? Okay... sure.' He hopped down from the barstool completely unsure of what was about to happen.

I dragged him to the inconspicuous dance floor and glued myself to his chest. When he didn't complain, I took things far beyond the level of propriety normally upheld at a tame, family-friendly Indian bar.

'I think your friends are getting angry.' He whispered into my ear after about half an hour of vertical foreplay.

'Huh?' I opened my eyes and dimly recalled the occasion of a bachelorette party, the naughty lingerie, whips and handcuffs that my friends and I had wrapped so carefully in expensive silk. The same friends who were now standing next to the walls like a pack of hungry hounds. I ignored their hostility and rushed to apologise to the bride-to-be. 'Where is Anubha?' I slurred and then felt a little guilty.

'In the toilet, crying,' replied my best friend who has known me to be flaky and amoral since we were ten.

'Why is she crying?'

'She says she doesn't want to get married.'

'The usual then...' I brushed her off and sashayed back to my beau de jour.

'Why doesn't your friend want to get married? She said yes... non?'

'I think I'm going to kiss you.'

'Oh okay... but your frie—'

He never finished the sentence. We stood there in the middle of the bar, sucking on each other's tongues till two familiar arms pulled me away from the crime scene and pushed me into the elevator.

'NO!' The door closed on his receding face and I thought I heard him say, 'Come back... I must see you again.' Perhaps it was meant to be a request but it struck me like a command.

In the caffeine haze of the morning after, I found his text, which contained a simple invitation for a holiday. How he discovered my number is a mystery yet to be solved. 'I finish my project next week. Then I have four days off. So you and me, anywhere you want to go if you come see me in Pune.'

The smile vanished from my face. I cupped my breasts and peered into the bathroom mirror. Four nights? Too long for a one-night stand; too short for an affaire de coeur. Then there was also the wedding, the first one in our coterie. I must see you again, the words echoed in my head, *I must see you again.* It was the slightest thing. If he had said, I want to see you again or I would like to see you again, I would've deposited him in my vast repository of 'maybes'. But the *must* got to me in the end. I booked my tickets and declared a family emergency.

'But what about Anubha's wedding?' My best friend turned her haggard face towards me; she knows everyone in my family.

'You said she doesn't want to get married... maybe she won't.'

'If that's in the stars... maybe.'

'Has she even... at the very least...you know... kissed the man she doesn't want to marry?'

'Like you kissed that French boy?'

'What does that mean?' I was annoyed.

'Exactly, it means nothing. A kiss is just a kiss, it doesn't make a marriage.'

'Ok-kay.' There was no point in arguing, so I shut up and left.

My anticipation barely made it through security and was much too big for the skinny overhead compartment. Somewhere in transit, I received another text, the address of my final destination; a swanky five-star hotel in the heart of Koregaon Park. The idea of fucking in a hotel unsettled me, the whole proposition suddenly looked dirty and boring. That is, till I saw him ambling towards me with the same shy smile on his face. He seemed just as uncomfortable as my insides; at least we were in this together.

'Coucou ca va? Let me take your bag.' The elevator closed with a bell, he pressed his lips against mine and we were back at that night. The days in between had dissolved into the ether.

'I've missed your beautiful lips... I've missed you...' We

walked to the room, hand in hand. It was messy. His clothes were everywhere; his six pairs of shoes were wedged between the sofa and the bed.

'Is this okay? I didn't want to clean.' He asked as though he had organised the mess on purpose. Perhaps he had, there was a hint of thoughtfulness on his face. I didn't feel like I was in a hotel anymore.

'That's alright.'

'Is this bed okay? It's not very big... we can change the room if you like,' he said politely. But I failed to register a word after *bed*, which was gaping at us like the elephant in the room.

'Hmm... should we try it and see?' I suggested bashfully and stretched out on the mountain of pillows. Standing at the edge, he looked more petrified than aroused but followed me anyway. The mattress dipped under his weight. He crawled over me on all fours and peered into my face. I expected us to kiss again but nothing happened. He continued to hover over me and I continued to breathe heavily.

'Aren't you tired?' His finger skimmed my cheek and traced the edge of my collarbone.

'A little bit, yes.'

'Would you like to eat something?'

'Sure.'

He immediately reached for the phone but I stopped him and pulled him to the side.

'Maybe after a few minutes?'

'Okay.'

The tension fizzled out as soon as I put my head on his shoulder. He drew me closer and I threw my leg over his hips.

He smelled like a densely wooded hillside, filled with secret, exotic flowers.

'Are you sleeping?' I nudged him with my elbow.

'No, just want to hold you for a bit,' he said. As I circled my fingers over the mole on his left shoulder and the tiny hair on his chest, something stirred deep inside of me. Something entirely asexual and accompanied by the lilting voice of Billie Holiday. *Just like the sting of a bee, you turned the tables on me... and now I'm falling for you.*

Be still, you reckless heart!

I decided to end the cuddling right away and descended down his chest, kissing the hollow between his ribs and the protrusion of his hipbone. He laughed when I licked his navel and trembled when I nuzzled the space where his thighs connected to his torso.

'Stop, stop, you're killing me! We have four days. What's the rush?'

'I don't understand... don't you want to have sex with me?'

'Of course, I do.'

We remained quiet for a while.

'I like your dress. You look good in blue.'

'Hmm.' I tried my best not to look at him. He lifted my hips and pulled down my plain cotton underwear. I remained unaffected. He kissed, sucked, licked and fucked me with his tongue, he did everything right but I couldn't enjoy it. I came twice, he continued to swivel his tongue but I still couldn't relax.

'What's wrong? Are you okay?'

'Yes, I'm fine. Let's have sex.'

'We just did.'

'When?'

'Right now...'

'But you didn't...'

'So what?'

'That's not sex!'

'It's not?'

The question hung over my head like a bright new incandescent bulb. What exactly was my definition of sex? Where did it start? Where did it end? Staring into his warm brown eyes, I realised that I didn't know the most important thing about the man who had just upset the very foundation of my adult life.

'What is your name?'

'You don't remember? I told you that night.'

'Sorry, I was too drunk to remember,' I confessed, feeling ashamed of myself.

'Merde! Hahaha.'

The bed shook with his laughter. It thrilled me to see him like this. It was almost as good as seeing him come. The laughter slowly turned into smiles. He touched my face and I touched his. The whole thing was sex, right from the laughter to the way his eyes lit up when he looked at me. In between kisses, I fleetingly thought about other men, the ones I'd had sex with and the ones I'd simply allowed to sleep in the same bed. I also thought about Anubha, perched on top of a gilded stool under the bright lights of a video camera, accompanied by the ancient chants of stoic pandits. Would she ever find real sex or would she spend her life quietly assuming that it was all in the stars?

About the Contributors

Aditya Sharma studied Law at Delhi University and then practised in his hometown for a couple of years—until he discovered he wanted to be a writer. He started off by freelancing for several national newspapers and magazines. When a weekly publication took him on as a journalist in Delhi, he was more than relieved to be rescued from a lawyer's drab life in the district courts. He has since then worked with several magazines including the *Reader's Digest* and also written for *The Hindu, The Tribune, Sahara Time* and *Life Positive*. A Mumbai-based writer, *Champs of Devgarh* is his first novel.

Amitava Kumar is the author of several works of nonfiction and a novel. His writing has appeared in *Granta, Harper's, Caravan, The Guardian,* and *The New York Times*. He teaches English at Vassar College in upstate New York.

Amrita Chatterjee started her writing career at a very early age, two years old to be precise, and drove her parents to bankruptcy by scribbling all over the walls with permanent markers. And now, two decades later, not much has changed. She is the author of *Special Lassi,* the account of a wild, psychedelic romp across the Himalayas, and lives in New Delhi with a money plant that refuses to die despite being watered once a month.

Arunava Sinha is an award-winning translator of classic, modern and contemporary Bengali writing. He has contributed significantly to the presence of a number of fine Bengali writers in English, including Buddhadev Bose, Rabindranath Tagore and Sankar.

Cyrus Mistry is a playwright, short-story writer and novelist. For nearly twenty years he regularly wrote feature articles, book and film reviews for prominent newspapers and magazines in the country. He has also authored several screenplays and documentary film scripts, some of which have been successfully made into films. He divides his time between Mumbai and Kodaikanal.

Jaishree Misra has written eight novels and edited an anthology of writings on motherhood. She has a Master's degree in English Literature from Kerala University and two post-graduate diplomas from the University of London, in Special Education and Broadcast. She presently lives in Kerala.

Kankana Basu is a Mumbai-based writer and illustrator. She is a book critic for various publications such as *The Sunday Hindu, The Asian Age* and *The New Indian Express*. She is the author of *Vinegar Sunday* (a collection of short stories), *Cappuccino Dusk* (a novel long-listed for the 2007 Man Asian Prize) and *Lamplight: Paranormal Stories from the Hinterlands*. She illustrates children's fiction and assists in the translation work of her grandfather, the late Bengali author Saradindu Bandopadhyay.

Krishna Shastri Devulapalli is a cartoonist, children's illustrator, graphic designer, columnist and writer. He has written two novels, *Ice Boys in Bell-bottoms* and *Jump Cut*, and a play, *Dear Anita*. His latest book is called *How to Be a Literary Sensation: A Quick*

Guide to Exploiting Friends, Family & Facebook for Financial Gain. This is his first foreplay into the realm of erotica.

Kristen Cosby is a teacher, editor and international vagabond. When not travelling, she lives and works in San Francisco.

Meena Kandasamy is a writer based in Chennai. She has published two collections of poetry and a novel, *The Gypsy Goddess*.

Mitali Saran is a freelance writer and columnist based in Delhi. She has sniggered at enough badly written sex to know better than to try writing erotica; and yet here she is, because, well, you should try everything once.

Rupa Bajwa is is the author of two novels – *The Sari Shop* and *Tell Me a Story*. *The Sari Shop* was long-listed for the Orange Prize for Fiction, and went on to win the XXIV Grinzane Cavour award for best first novel, the Commonwealth Award, and the Sahitya Akademi Award. Rupa also writes book reviews and articles on other interests in *The Telegraph*, *The Tribune* and *India Today*. She divides her time between Amritsar and various other Indian cities and towns (the way writers do between Delhi, London and New York). Her third novel will be published soon.

Shinie Antony has written four short-story books, including *The Orphanage for Words* and *Barefoot & Pregnant*. Her novels include *When Mira Went Forth and Multiplied* and *A Kingdom for His Love*. Co-founder of the Bangalore Literature Festival, she won the Commonwealth Short Story Asia region prize in 2003 for her story *A Dog's Death*.

Born and educated mostly in Gaya, Bihar, **Tabish Khair** is a poet, novelist and critic. He has won the All India Poetry Prize and his fiction has been widely translated and short-listed for major awards. His latest novel, *Jihadi Jane*, has been released in India, UK and USA. He lives and teaches in Denmark now.

Taslima Nasrin, an award-winning novelist, celebrated memoirist, physician, secular humanist and human rights activist, is known for her powerful writing on women's oppression and unflinching criticism of religion, despite forced exile and multiple fatwas calling for her death. Her thirty-seven books have been translated into thirty languages. Her works have won her the prestigious Ananda Puraskar in 1992 and 2000. She has bagged the Sakharov Prize for Freedom of Thought from the European Parliament, the Kurt Tucholsky Award from the Swedish PEN, the Simone de Beauvoir Prize and numerous other awards and doctorates.

Vikram Kapur is the author of two critically acclaimed novels. His short fiction and nonfiction have been published in various Indian and international publications. His short stories have been shortlisted in several international competitions including, among others, the Commonwealth Short Story Prize and the Fish International Short Story Prize. He is Associate Professor of English at Shiv Nadar University.